Phil Redmond

HOLLYOAKS
A MERSEY TELEVISION COMPANY

STOLEN
E-MAILS

Phil Redmond's

HOLLYOAKS
A MERSEY TELEVISION COMPANY

STOLEN
E-MAILS

chris parker

4 BOOKS

First published 2001 by Channel 4 Books
an imprint of Pan Macmillan Ltd
Pan Macmillan, 20 New Wharf Road, London N1 9RR
Basingstoke and Oxford
Associated companies throughout the world
www.panmacmillan.com

ISBN 0 752 21955 3

3 5 7 9 8 6 4 2

A CIP catalogue record for this book is available from
the British Library.

Photographs © The Mersey Television Company Limited
Designed and typeset by Ben Cracknell Studios
Printed and bound by Mackays of Chatham plc, Chatham, Kent

This book accompanies the television series *Hollyoaks* made by
The Mersey Television Company for Channel 4.
Series Producer: Jo Hallows
Executive Producer: Phil Redmond

15 April 2001   10:50pm

I need to sleep. My eyes sting from the monitor and my brain feels
bruised. I've got that late-night hunger which tells you you've
been up too long, but I can't risk a fridge raid and all I've got is a
wilted slice of pepperoni pizza. A few streets away, I can hear the
Chester homeboys parked outside the chip shop blasting Eminem
from their car stereo. Well, everyone has their own idea of fun.
Welcome to mine.

> To: Mandy
> From: Ben
> Subject: Born 2 do it
>
> All right gorgeous
> I had to bribe Margaret with a chocolate chip muffin for two
> minutes on the office computer, so I hope you appreciate it... Being
> stuck in a fire station with no one to talk to but the lads gives me an
> overheated imagination. Since I started my shift, I've been thinking
> about coming to see you tonight. Have a corkscrew ready, cos I'm
> going to bring some wine up to your room. We'll get nicely drunk
> and mellow, and then I'm going to take off whatever you're wearing
> and kiss you till you can't stand it (*especially* there). Then we'll do it
> all night in slo-mo. Interested? (Don't reply to that, Margaret's on
> her way over with choc chips in her teeth.)
> Ben XXX(rated)

OK, so I'm officially a *bad* person. Because if you had the chance to
read your friends' most intimate thoughts, you'd turn it down and
hurry back to your nice, safe existence, wouldn't you? *Yeah, right.*

I know I'm close. I have to be. I return to the sign-in screen of Lewis's mail server. It's the second night I've spent trying to think my way into his mind, and there's no way I'm giving up now. *Think.*

theloft	Please re-enter password
ruthosborne	Please re-enter password
lorraine	Please re-enter password
ihatevictoria	Please re-enter password
mandyrichardson	Please re-enter password
marketstall	Password accepted

I'm in. Fireworks go off in my brain. Ten thousand spectators do a Mexican wave. It's the best feeling in the world. (Yes, better than *anything*. OK, maybe I've just led a sheltered life, but for me at least, it's the truth.)

I feel a bit dizzy, slightly sick. It's like Christmas morning when you're a kid and you don't know what to open first. There are hundreds of messages here, some of them more than a year old. Where do I go first? I scan the list. Problem solved…

To: Lewis
From: Finn
Subject: Izzy dances for you naked

So I've finally got your attention have I? If you get this, you're sitting in a web-café somewhere on your travels. While you're off finding yourself – thanks for telling me what you're up to, by the way – spare a thought for those of us trying to keep our business afloat. Get onto the people who supply us with DJs and make sure we've got their top talent on the nights when Izzy is doing warm-up. Because frankly, the girl DJs like tortoises shag. I have to stop myself going to give her a hand. Also, she has a secret mystery formula that I'm starting to suss. The other night it was all Aphex Twin, Ash, Aerosmith. Last night she kicked off with the Baha Men and Britney. Notice a pattern emerging? Still – I can't wait till she gets to double D…
Finn

To: Finn
From: Lewis
Subject: Re: Izzy dances for you naked

You took her on without consulting me, as I remember. Why keep her if she's so bad?

To: Lewis
From: Finn
Subject: Re: Izzy dances for you naked

She's fit. She's horny. She's non-ugly. She puts a spring in an old man's step. She's easy on the eye – in fact, she gives your pupils a fortnight on a sun-bed in Marbella. Do you see where I'm going with this?

To: Finn
From: Lewis
Subject: Re: Izzy dances for you naked

Right. Well, I think you should discuss this with Victoria. I'm sure she'd understand.

I send 'Izzy dances for you naked' to the girl herself. I admit – having that power gives me a buzz. But I have to be careful. Every time I pull a stunt like that I'm increasing the chances of getting caught, and there's no way I can let that happen. If anyone finds out who I am and what I'm doing, I'm dead. Or I might as well be.

To: Ruth
From: Lewis
Subject: Us

Yikes! Was there ever a stronger contender for scariest e-mail title? But it's like driving past a car crash and I can't look away. I even feel a teeny pang of guilt at spying on the wreckage of this couple's relationship. On second thoughts, I think it's just hunger. Well, here goes...

Hi

How are you? OK, silly question and I don't expect you to answer it.
I'm having a coffee in Belfast. I just wanted to say that I left Chester
to get my head together and it seems to be working. The weird
thing is, the further I get from you, the more I think about
everything that happened. Maybe it's spending time on my own. But
I know if I was face-to-face with you I wouldn't have the guts to say
this.

Ruth, out of all the things I've done which have hurt you, there's
one I can't stop thinking about – even worse (if that's possible) than
being unfaithful with Lorraine. I know you know what I mean. I just
want you to know it's the first thought in my mind when I wake up,
and it probably always will be. And the worst part is that I tried to
use your guilt to excuse what I'd done. When I fell down the Loft
steps, I let you think you'd pushed me, like you were getting me
back for what I did to you. I know you'd never hurt me deliberately,
because you'd never sink to my level. I want you to know I will
never stop punishing myself.

I don't know if saying this will do either of us any good. If I was
wrong to send it, just delete it.

Lewis

I don't understand this. I knew it wouldn't be pretty, but something
about this really spooks me. What could have been 'worse than
Lorraine'? I check through Lewis's inbox, but I can't find a reply from
Ruth.

See what I mean by power though? A couple of keystrokes and
this could be on its way to Lewis's entire address book. For what
feels like the thousandth time, I try to break into Ruth's account.

newspaper	Please re-enter password
superscoop	Please re-enter password
ilovejournalism	Please re-enter password

I try twenty more names, using every bit of information I know about
Ruth: relationship disaster with Lewis, studying for PhD, fancies
herself as the next Kate Adie, has please-just-do-it-if-you're-going-

to-do-it sexual tension thing going with Taylor… and that's about it. This girl never gives too much away. Which must be why she chose a password that really works. This is starting to bug me.

I should log off. My body's screaming at me to put it under the duvet and leave it alone for eight hours – but sorry, not possible. I *have* to know what Lewis meant. I bring up Finn's account – finn@deadgoodmail.com. The only mail referring to Lewis is from months ago, just before the wedding.

> To: Carol
> From: Finn
> Subject: Vic, Lewis and You
>
> I'll keep it brief, cos I know you'd much rather be having cocktails at the captain's table (or whatever you do on cruise ships) than chewing the fat with the likes of me. The thing is, since I've been back from Barcelona, a lot of stuff's been bothering me. Stuff between us. Especially what you said about not saying goodbye when you set off round the world. I'm sorry about loads of things, but that's at the top of the heap. Seeing you reminded me of how I've missed our chats. So if you get this and have a few idle moments, I'd really like it if we could stay in touch. So this is sort of goodbye (for the time I should've said it) and hello (hopefully, for the future).
>
> One thing I never really got to find out is what you think of Victoria. That's you as in Carol, not you as in Tony's friend. I ask this because Lewis can't stand her and it's starting to get to me. Sounds dead old-fashioned, I know, but if you could give us your blessing it'd mean a lot to me. I'll need all the support I can get on the big day.
> Finn
> PS Where are you? I got a cool, old globe from a house clearance last week. I'll look you up.

> To: Finn
> From: Carol
> Subject: Re: Vic, Lewis and You

It's a bit late, but yeah, I wouldn't mind us exchanging the odd
e-mail, just to remind me what I'm not missing. Finn, if you want
me to tell you that you're doing the right thing, just say.
Carol
PS Just passing Ustica, a few miles north of Sicily.

To: Carol
From: Finn
Subject: Re: Vic, Lewis and You

I want you to tell me that I'm doing the right thing.
Finn
PS Aha. Gotcha. Well, have a great time.

To: Finn
From: Carol
Subject: Re: Vic, Lewis and You

OK, whatever.
Carol
PS I am doing.

This sounds more promising...

To: Finn
From: Ruth
Subject: Lewis

Finn, I don't want to pry into your business, but is there a reason
why Lewis has suddenly taken off on this trip? He seemed very
strained last time I spoke to him.
    I tried to talk to Helen but she was really odd with me. It seems
like whatever he does, we're the ones who end up losing sleep
over it.
Ruth

To: Ruth
From: Finn
Subject: Re: Lewis

He's buying stock for the yard. That's the official reason. Why he decided to go so soon is anyone's guess. You know more about him than me. Which is possibly not very much at all. I've given up trying to work out what he's up to.

I hate to say this about my best mate, but it's a relief to have him out of the way for a while. It's a lot easier when I've only got myself to argue with.

Want to talk more at the Dog? Say, eight o'clock?

Finn

To: Finn
From: Ruth
Subject: Re: Lewis

Please.
See you
Ruth

Only one other e-mail catches my eye.

To: Finn, Lewis, O.B., Tony, Ben, Luke
From: Keeper of Stag Laws
Subject: Rules of the Stag

1. Tell no one what went on.
2. Post all stag-related messages in encrypted file.
3. Never reveal the password.
4. Tell no one what went on.

Strange how it wasn't sent to all the lads who went on the stag night, only a select few. There's an attachment underneath which can't be read without a password. It all seems a bit less impressive when I notice it came from Max Cunningham's e-mail address, but still, I really want to know what they got up to. For now, I need a fast and easy route to Planet Lewis. I go back to Mandy's account (which was a no-brainer to crack. Friendly advice: be suspicious of people asking to use your server because theirs is 'down' and they suddenly have to send an urgent e-mail).

To: Cindy
From: Mandy
Subject: Lewis

Hi Cind

Hope you and Holly are OK… Have you heard from your dad? This is my subtle way of asking whether he's said anything to you about my dear brother. He's gone off on some 'business trip' which he suddenly decided was really urgent. I've spoken to Finn, but he didn't give much away. Every time I mention it to Mum she gets really edgy and defensive, so there's no point pushing it. Weird isn't it – we used to be really close and now I'm trying to find out about him from my step-sister in Spain. Well, if you hear anything…

Two other bits of news, but they're kind of linked. I had a driving test booked (don't laugh) which I couldn't make (long story). I don't really know how to put this – I haven't told anyone else – Laura took the test in my name and passed. The first I knew about it was when she turned up with the pass certificate. How bizarre is that? I was seriously freaked out. I turned it down, but I still played along with the idea this was somehow a normal thing to do.

Oh, and Laura is now 'seeing' Luke. I'm totally fine about it, but she's been a bit off with me since they got together. I feel like she wants to draw a line under me and Luke – as if she needed to.
Love
Mandy XXX

To: Mandy
From: Cindy
Subject: Freaky

She did WHAT? Are you serious? All I can say is I'd be running away screaming by now.

Think about it though – you could've turned down your only hope of getting a licence. (Only kidding!)

I'd keep her at arms' length for a while and see if she turns into a full-on mentalist before you let her become your best buddy. You *sure* you're OK about her and Luke?
Take care.
Love Cindy

I want to find out more about Laura, she's always seemed a bit weird to me, but I'm in danger of going off on a serious tangent here. Lewis is tonight's mission. I'd better not push my luck, though. I log off. Once the computer shuts down, I'm in total silence. Even the chip shop posse has found somewhere better to be.

I'm logging back on. Lewis has me hooked. I trawl through again, searching for anything that stands out from the mass of e-mails to and from Finn and Ruth. I choose the most random, dull-sounding title I can find – you never know. Four or five e-mails in, I hit this.

To: Driver and Vehicle Licensing Agency
From: Lewis
Subject: Enquiry

Dear Sir or Madam
I have recently changed my address. Please could you tell me what documents you need so you can update my licence?
Kurt Benson

Kurt Benson. As in, Ruth's former husband. As in, died two years ago. As in, what the hell is Lewis doing with his driving licence? I get this cold sensation over my scalp and down my neck. It's like that saying: *Someone just walked over my grave.* Get a grip.

Think. Is there any legitimate reason why Lewis would have this licence? Some kind of favour to Ruth? Come on – what, is he going to have it *framed* for her? This is definitely dodgy. He made no attempt to hide his e-mail address, but then no one's going to care – it's only an enquiry after all. I check the date. 25 March 2001. Just before Lewis set off on his business trip.

I wind the string on my yo-yo and let it go into the shadow beside the desk, where I can see the little lights come on as it spins. It slips from my fingers and falls into the empty computer box that I haven't got round to throwing out. The computer – that's what started all this. When I bought this top-of-the-range toy, I got myself a whole new life. I can escape to a place where I'm totally free. My biggest fear is that one day, I'll have to leave. It's like a super-addictive drug: one hit was all it took to get me hooked. Once I'd experienced the rush of getting inside people's heads, I knew I'd have to go back for that feeling again and again.

What I should do now is log off and forget I've seen what I had no right to be looking at in the first place. But even I don't buy that. What I should do is come clean and tell Ruth. I see her nearly every day, after all. But that would mean the end of all this, and the end of me. No one loves a cybersnoop. No one would ever trust me again. OK, so I could forward this e-mail to her and stay anonymous. Let her get on with her own inquiries. But the truth is, now I've got the scent, it kills me to think of anyone else sussing Lewis before I do. I close the e-mail and scroll down, working my way through each e-mail, careful I don't miss the tiniest thing. I scavenge through joke attachments from Finn (I can't believe people are still wasting time downloading that monkey sniffing its own turd), messages to suppliers, notes to Victoria and a whole load of other irrelevant junk, until blinking is like opening and closing Velcro. And there's so much more to get through.

I hear a door shut. Someone's come out onto the landing. I log off. But before I've got as far as shutting down, I'm typing lewisr@speedymail.com. I get as far as inputting his password before I force myself to stop. *Get a grip.*

marketstall

Nice touch. Very down-to-earth for someone with a dead man's driving licence in his pocket. A man who remembers where he came from. The question is, where is he going?

17 April 2001   1:49am

Two people remarked on my appearance today. (Got to admit that 'two burnt holes in a bloody sheet' (© Chloe Bruce) was a pretty accurate description of my eyes.) This means I either have to cut down on my screen time or get some better eyedrops, otherwise people will start to wonder about me. First things first – to Finn's inbox. I've got to see if there's a response from Izzy.

To: Finn
From: Izzy
Subject: Re: Izzy dances for you naked

I'm trying to work out who's more pathetic. You, for writing this Year Eight drivel, or Lewis, for being so computer-inept that he forwarded it to me. Either way, the whole idea about making juvenile remarks about people behind their backs is that it's supposed to be *behind their backs*. If, on the other hand, you have a complaint about my work, this should be addressed to my face. I thought Victoria would have been able to muster up the necessary balls, even though you and Lewis obviously can't.

Please don't flatter yourself into thinking I'm offended. Use the time to find another DJ.
Izzy

To: Izzy
From: Finn
Subject: grovel

What can I say? Lewis may be a buffoon, but I'm entirely to blame for this. It was just a desperate and, yes, pathetic attempt to raise a laugh from my humourless colleague. We both really value your work. Please don't desert us in our time of need. Get in touch and maybe we can talk about extending your set.
Finn

To: Finn
From: Izzy
Subject: Re: grovel

I'll take three hours, with a 50% increase in pay.
Yours non-negotiably
Izzy

To: Lewis
From: Finn
Subject: You gormless tit

Take a good, hard look at the attached file and start concocting the
explanation of your life. This got back to Izzy *how*, exactly? I've only
had to agree to give her an extra hour to stop her walking, you
complete nutsack. Good to see you're doing so much for employee
relations, even while you can't be with us.
Finn

Now I'm worried. What if Finn's message to Lewis has prompted him
to spring-clean his files? If he's been through deleting Finn's old
e-mails, chances are he's also wiped out anything vaguely
incriminating or even changed his password. I brace myself and hack
into Lewis's account, praying silently: please don't let me have blown
it all for the sake of a cheap laugh. I *have* to get inside his life.

Once I'm in, I check to see if Lewis has replied. Nothing. None of his
e-mails has been touched since my smash and grab last night. I go
straight to the e-mail from Finn and delete it, then clear it permanently
from the 'deleted mail' file. I'm itching to continue rooting through his
mail where I left off last night, but this narrow escape has made me
jumpy and I don't want to hang around in here. Just as I'm about to
exit, I notice some really old mail from Izzy, but it's only one of those
cheesy questionnaires you're supposed to fill in and pass on to annoy
your friends.

To: Lewis, Finn, Adam, Chloe, Anna, Alex, O.B., Max
From: Izzy
Subject: Twenty questions

What time is it?	1:05pm
Name as it appears on your birth certificate:	Isabel Octavia Cornwell
Nickname at school:	Izzers, Zabel
Pets:	Marmaduke, Weevil, Stinker, Snowy
Piercings:	I *don't* think so
Tattoos:	Ditto

Been to how many continents?	All of them
Dumper or dumpee?	Dumper
Favourite place to be kissed:	Grandpa's summerhouse
Talker or listener?	Listener
Most annoying trait in others:	Lack of manners
Fantasy partner:	Ralph Fiennes
Most embarrassing incident:	Meeting Ralph Fiennes at garden party and mispronouncing his name
Fighter or lover?	Both, when I have to be
Favourite position:	Sorry?
Proudest moment:	Winning regional point-to-point, 1998
Favourite word:	Outstanding
Biggest fear:	Mediocrity
Loved somebody so much it made you cry?	Yes
If yes, who?	As if

I have to bite my hand to keep myself from laughing out loud. *Listener?* And it's the first time I've ever heard it called *Grandpa's summerhouse*. She's given me an idea, though. I get onto the homepage of her mail server.

snowy	Password not accepted
stinker	Password not accepted
weevil	Password not accepted
marmaduke	Password accepted

Bingo. An animal's name. For a posh girl like Izzy it just had to be, didn't it? I wish I'd stumbled upon this earlier. It would've saved all those attempts to crack her password with the likes of *frostymadam* and *snobbybird*. I choose one of the earliest of her sent items.

To: Sis-sis
From: Izzy
Subject: This place

God, I hate to admit it but you were so right, I should've sat my A-levels again and applied for Exeter. This place is *so* much worse than I expected. They don't even know how to organise a proper pool party. Don't tell Mummy and Boo-Boo, but I would have drowned if it hadn't been for this boy who pulled me out (too ghastly to go into details). His name's Adam Morgan and his dad's a chip-fryer or something at this random little café, but he's rather cute. He asked me for a date and I nearly said 'OK, 1995, or whenever that Liam Gallagher hair of yours was in fashion', but I remembered your lecture about how my mouth gets me into trouble and smiled sweetly. Anyway, we're going out tomorrow night (probably to eat pies or play darts or something). The only cloud on the horizon is this person called 'Geri' (mmm, classy spelling). How do I sum her up without being unnecessarily cruel? You know the stuff you see in designer shops at sale time and you think, who on earth actually wears this kind of thing? That person is Geri. Anyway, I think she and Adam had a thing for about five seconds, months ago, and she can't get over it… Wish me luck.
Hugs
Iz

Thank you Marmaduke, whoever you are, whatever you are. (Pony? Horse? I'm guessing not a hamster.) *How* desperate am I to forward this little beauty to Geri and Adam? This desperate: I get as far as typing in Geri's address before sanity returns. *Way* too dangerous. I keep scrolling through the collected works of Izzy until I find something more recent.

To: Sis-sis
From: Izzy
Subject: Adam

You will not believe what Adam has done, Bella. We've all found out he's installed hidden cameras throughout the house and he's been filming *everything*. Apparently it was 'essential' that we weren't to know what was going on – he says it's for his end-of-year project – but guess who was in on it? *Correct.* Suddenly a lot of odd situations start to make sense, like the time she went all lipstick-lesbian on me. Adam was pulling her strings for weeks, persuading her to make me look stupid. Well, it certainly worked. I kept it together long enough to tell him we were finished but I just feel hollow and so humiliated. I can't believe he could do this to me.

I honestly don't think he ever really cared for me. How could he, when all this time he's been plotting with *her*? I told her she was a sad, desperate character who was trying to cling onto Adam, but I think there's more to it than that. I think the last few months have been this huge flirt-fest between the two of them. I was just roped in by Adam to make Geri so jealous she'd want him ten times more than he ever did when they were together. It really hurts because I genuinely liked him. How could I have been so *thick*?

I'm trying to see it as a lesson. Never, *ever*, get involved with anyone who has unfinished business. I could really do with a chat and perhaps a bit of a boo-hoo. Can you be somewhere near your phone 5pm UK time?

Iz

I'm torn between continuing with Izzy or switching over to her arch-enemy's account. (Another trusting soul. I saw her password – *gstring* – scribbled on the cover of her copy of *Film Theory and Criticism,* right alongside her e-mail address.)

To: Anna
From: Geri
Subject: That girl

I'm in the media lab and I think I'm going to explode if IC looks at me one more time like I just fell out from under her horse's tail. Adam was in here a minute ago. He came over to talk to me and she immediately had to interrupt, just in case I leapt on him. Then she said something 'funny' and he almost lost control of his bladder. How is it possible for someone to have such a total personality collapse in such a short space of time? Still, at least when I see him fawning over her it makes me realise I'm not interested anyway.

Geri

PS Had a really weird dream about being in a forest and waking up next to this tree that was covered in fungus. What does your book say?

To: Geri
From: Anna
Subject: Re: That girl

I'd like to believe you about Adam but I don't think I do...

Give Izzy a chance. I think she feels a bit insecure and she's trying to overcompensate. She'll calm down when she settles in.

Anna

PS Were you alone in the forest? If so, the book reckons you may be let down by someone you've been relying on. Fungus is supposed to mean you have hostile competition that you have to fight against.

To: Anna
From: Geri
Subject: Re: That girl

Anna, there's generosity and there's having a screw loose. How much more 'settled in' could she be? I went away and all the signs from Adam were that he wanted us to be together. I come back to find he's been taken over by a blonde mop with a plum in its mouth and two basketballs stuck to it. And I'm supposed to see a silver lining in this *how*, exactly?

Geri

PS Right. So not accurate at all then?!

To: Chloe, Anna
From: Geri
Subject: Izzy-isms

Send in your favourite sayings and quirks from the queen of irritation! List updated regularly.

'You bought it second hand? How do you know no one died in it?' (To Alex, re his jacket)

'I'm tired of all this bickering over who does what. Can't we just get a cleaner in?' (To fellow tenants in Tony's house)

'So you and Matt are seeing each other?' ('Yes') 'Do you find enough to talk about, with him being a caretaker?' (To Chloe)

'I find it quite hard to get clothes that fit because I'm skinny, but my boobs are quite big.' (To entire canteen. Let's start a charity fund: Perfect Body Aid.)

'Don't you think it's a shame that Sophie Dahl has lost weight? She used to make such a refreshing change, didn't she?' (To Chloe)

'What's the number to phone orders through to the canteen?' (To Alex, who gave her the number of the principal's office, little devil)

My first instinct is to send this to everyone I know, but it'd make Izzy ask too many questions. I can't believe this hasn't already found its way back to her, though. I go back to her account but I can't see it. I browse through a few of her messages before finding this...

To: Sis-sis
From: Izzy
Subject: I'm a gangsta bitch, yo

Well, you said Chester would broaden my horizons, but I'm not sure if this is what you had in mind... Your baby sis is now a rap promoter! Oh, did I mention I'm also co-owner of a label? I know, it's completely mad! These two local lads, Max and O.B., have put together a track – 'Get Down with That Thing' (don't ask) – including a sample from one of their dads (!). It gives new depths to the word pitiful. But Theo, the cool Zen guy I told you about, thinks there's a market for this kind of thing among us oh-so 'ironic' students.

As for the lads themselves, neither is the sharpest suit on the rack but Max is sort of sweet, if a little bit dopey. He really thinks this is a way out of his hopeless, dole-boy existence and I almost feel sorry for him. The other one, 'O.B.' (which I assume is some kind of 'rap' name he's invented) is a cocky, runty, little chancer. God, it's just struck me who he looks like – remember there was that slightly simple stable boy grandpa had to let go because they caught him in the ladies' at the horse trials? I *swear* O.B.'s his twin!

So *no*, Bella, before you ask – business and pleasure will not be
overlapping this time.
Hugs
Iz

I've always thought O.B.'s ego needed taking down a few sizes, so I
forward this to him. But I still haven't got any further with Lewis. I
bring up the welcome screen of his mail-server, but hesitate before
typing in the password. I've built this up so much in my own mind
that I'm actually nervous. This is crazy. What's the worst that could
happen?

I spend ten minutes digging patiently through the dross before I
stumble upon this.

To: Dennis Richardson, c/o HMP Blackwood
From: Lewis
Subject: (No subject)

I've done something you'd be proud of. Yeah, if you'd have seen me
you'd have smiled and thought 'good lad, he's turning out just like
me' – well, I'm NOT.
    Yes, I'm off my face in case you're wondering, in the office with
half a bottle of scotch and a load of beer, but that's another one I've
learnt from you, isn't it, Dad? Do it in style and in SECRET. I hope
you burn in Hell. I hope you look at yourself in the morning and
want to kill yourself. But you'll never hate yourself as much as I
hate you.

To: Dennis Richardson, c/o HMP Blackwood
From: Lewis
Subject: (No subject)

I made a mistake, but don't ever think I'm turning out the way you
did. You have put your stain on me, I know that now, and I will never
forgive you for it. But at least I know it's there. Do you understand?
If I have to fight it every day of my life, no problem, I will. I'll never
forget what you did and I'll never let myself become what you are.

To: Dennis Richardson, c/o HMP Blackwood
From: Lewis
Subject: (No subject)

There's a big difference between us, Dad. You lied to yourself. I'm
being honest. I'm going to find every trace of you that's in me and get
rid of it. I'm sorting my life out. What I did will NEVER happen again.
You weren't capable of saying that. Or if you did, you lied.

Dead end. No more e-mails to the prison address. I'm struggling to
take this in. *Dennis Richardson*. Lewis has always been a jack-the-
lad, maybe capable of letting some dirty money change hands here
and there, but nothing serious. Yet here he is comparing himself to
his dad, a man who terrorised his wife and raped his daughter.

What can he have done? Nothing anywhere near as heavy as
that, surely. I'm not his biggest fan, but I'm pretty sure there's no
cruelty in him. Maybe it's just the alcohol messing with his mind.

I log off, but my mind's still logged on. Something even darker than I
suspected is going on beneath the surface of Lewis's life. *Hark at you,
Mulder.* Maybe I'm just spooking myself, getting caught up in the
drama of sitting here alone late at night, looking at things I shouldn't.
I log on and read that first e-mail – the drunk, scary one – again.
Somehow, I don't think so.

17 April 2001   6:28am

Well, *that* was a waste of time. Thanks to that lullaby from Lewis to his
father, I had a total of one hour's sleep max all night. I thought I'd get
up early to have a quick session before everyone else wakes up, so here
I am with a cup of tea and cornflakes.

I cruise Lewis's messages again, but nothing new has been
added. I don't know why it should be a surprise that he hasn't been
online between 1am and 6am. I promise myself I won't be on for
longer than twenty minutes. I head for Mandy's messages.

To: Cindy
From: Mandy
Subject: Hello

Sorry I haven't been in touch for a while, college has been mad, especially with the website as well. Laura's been helping me. I've thought of asking her to become co-owner of the website (that's assuming it'll be worth owning one day), but I'm not sure. I don't know what it is but I still don't feel 100% about her. We're getting on pretty well but she never mentions Luke unless I do first. I know there's nothing wrong with that, but he's supposed to be her boyfriend now. Does she think I'll be jealous or something? I don't know. I can't help thinking that going out with Luke is supposed to prove something to me, like she's as good as I am, even though she's probably better if anything. Once or twice I've wondered if she'd be interested in him at all if he hadn't been out with me. Does that make me sound like a complete bitch? I've been bottling all of this up, as you've probably guessed. I can't say anything about it to Ben, cos he's Mr Jealousy at the best of times.

Anyway, what about you? You never seem to mention your love life these days… How's Holly doing? Give her a kiss from me and say hi to Jude.
Mandy

To: Mandy
From: Cindy
Subject: Re: Hello

Isn't that like me saying you're only going out with Ben because he used to be with me? I'm not being rude Mand, but I don't see why your opinion would be so important to Laura. You'll hate me for this but are you sure there's not a bit of you that's jealous?

I never mention my love life because you never ask! Mind you, there wasn't much to tell until, a few weeks ago, I met a guy called Pete (I know, not very Spanish, but then he is from Stoke) when I took Holly to the beach. He's tallish with short, dark dreads. He's been working at a bar over here for the last three years. I thought about helping him get a bar manager's job – one of Jude's places needs someone – but I don't want him to feel he has to stick with me out of gratitude. We're taking it nice and slow.

Jude is being Mrs Businesswoman and still loves it out here, though she's pining for chip butties and Dad's special gravy. Don't say anything to Dad, but things aren't brilliant between her and Benicio. I think she's semi-seeing Javier, the bloke she paid to fly me over from England. We still get on pretty well, but I really need to get my own place soon. Now she's got the money she wants to party every night and sometimes it's hard to find a quiet room for Holly to sleep in.

Jude's just come in from the pool. She says to say hi to Mum, Dad, Tom and Max. Oh, and Lewis. She wants to have Max (plus girlfriend, she says – he hasn't got one, has he??!) out for a week soon, but don't tell him yet or he'll never stop pestering.

Take care

Cindy

Then I do something I immediately regret. I forward Mandy's 'Mr Jealousy' e-mail to Ben. Then I get cold feet. I try to rescue the situation by cracking b_davies@easyfree.com. Once I'm in, I can delete it.

firefighter	Password not recognised

Too obvious. Think.

backdraft	Password not recognised

Too Hollywood. *Think*.

mandyrichardson	Password not recognised

Come *on*.

I carry on trying names for maybe ten minutes, until I feel queasy in the pit of my stomach. Perhaps this is a wake-up call from my conscience. A ten-foot high neon sign flashing 'You are sick.' All I know is that I really don't want to do this any more. I hate this room and these sessions sitting hunched with the curtains drawn. And I think I'm starting to hate myself. I log off. I want to get showered and dressed, then go and do my work and talk to my friends, just as if I was a normal person.

3 May 2001   2:05am

OK. So it wasn't so easy to keep away. But I've seen Mandy and Ben swapping tonsils several times since the e-mail, so maybe I've been a bit hard on myself. Lewis's 'business trip' has now lasted almost three weeks. If anyone knows where he is, they're doing a good job of hiding it. Finn, Ruth and Mandy seem completely clueless. But my first stop has to be Mandy's mail-server.

To: Mandy
From: Ben
Subject: Mr Jealousy

I know you're not exactly Bill Gates, but I thought you'd have learned how to avoid basic screw-ups like this. Or are you trying to tell me something?
    If Luke no longer has the hots for you then why did we bother to creep around all those times? I think it'd be pretty weird if I *wasn't* jealous, wouldn't it?
Ben

To: Cindy
From: Mandy
Subject: Ben

I can't believe you told Ben what I said about him being jealous! Did you really think I wouldn't find out? Why did you do it?
Mandy

To: Mandy
From: Cindy
Subject: Re: Ben

Mand, I never even mentioned it – what are you on about? You must have sent him the same e-mail by mistake or something. I can't believe you think I'd go behind your back like that. Why would I?
Cindy

To: Mandy
From: Ben
Subject: Your punishment

I might forgive you – depends what's in it for me. How about round to mine, half eight. Dad's working late and Abby's sleeping over somewhere. Bring that coconut massage oil we used the other night. And wear that well-naughty silky thing you had on at the weekend. Then I'll think about it. (PS this has cost me another choc chip muffin – how are you going to repay me?)
Ben

'I never even mentioned it' sounds like Cindy's still in touch with Ben. It never really occurred to me. I have another go at breaking into Ben's e-mail account and hit the back of the net after five minutes with *bendavies*. Very secure, huh?

To: Ben
From: Zara
Subject: Hello from your god-daughter!!!

Hi Ben!!
I haven't seen you for ages ☹ but think of you lots!! Steph's parents are away this Saturday and we're having a party at hers. I've told everyone about you and there are loads of people who want to meet you!! We'd love you to come!!! I know we can't buy alcohol but don't worry, you can bring as much as you want (beer, wine or spirits).
Lots and lots of love
Za ☺X☺X☺X☺X☺X☺X☺X☺

To: Ben, Abby, Lisa, Steph, Brian
From: Zara
Subject: Twenty questions

Fill this in and pass it on!! Luv, Za

What time is it?	12:15pm
Name as it appears on your birth certificate:	Zara Charlotte Morgan
Nickname at school:	Za
Pets:	Brian (only kidding Bri!!)
Piercings:	Ears, belly (removed – had blood poisoning and nearly died); the rest – that's for me to know…
Tattoos:	Yes please (saving for little red devil on left bum cheek)
Been to how many continents?	When Dad had decent job, four. Since Deva opened, two
Dumper or dumpee?	Dumper (sorry guys!!)
Favourite place to be kissed:	Small of my back☺!
Talker or listener?	Depends if you're boring
Most annoying trait in others:	Nagging when I'm watching TV
Fantasy partner:	Tim Wheeler of Ash :-}~~ (me drooling)
Most embarrassing incident:	Watching Steph dance to 'Who Let the Dogs Out' (should've been who let the boob out!! You so did Steph!! Steve Jones has a photo!!)
Fighter or lover?	Both are cool
Favourite position:	I always come out on top
Proudest moment:	Being welcomed into the house of God
Favourite word:	Dweeb
Biggest fear:	Double Physics with Eggy Grant
Loved somebody so much it made you cry?	Yes, and them too
If yes, who?	You wish

He doesn't seem to have filled it in, big surprise. What I'd really like to find out is how long the whole Ben and Mandy thing was going on before Luke sussed. I go back through Ben's oldest e-mails, but they all seem to be for Cindy.

To: Cindy
From: Ben
Subject: Hi

Hi, how are you doing? Hope Holly is well. I know I haven't been in touch for ages – sorry about that. Things were pretty awkward for a while. At least all that stuff is behind us now.
      The real reason I'm writing this is because there's something I need to tell you. Mandy and I are seeing each other. It's all happened quite fast, just in the last few weeks. It's been really difficult with Luke (basically he thought he was still on with Mandy) so I didn't want to say anything sooner. But I thought I'd let you know before you found out from someone else. I hope you're OK with it. I still think about you and Holly, and I want us to keep in touch.
Love
Ben

To: Ben
From: Cindy
Subject: Re: Hi

Mandy beat you to it. She told me last week. It's fine. Holly's doing well, learning loads of Spanish. Yeah, I'd like to keep in touch. I was never angry with you, just with myself and the way things turned out.
Take care
Cind

What does he mean by 'stuff' in that e-mail to Cindy? I dig back to the first e-mail Ben sent her.

To: Cindy
From: Ben
Subject: (No subject)

Been trying to ring you all day. They haven't found anyone yet. Went back to the spot, but couldn't see anything. They could have got up and walked away. Took the car back to T's house but should've left it where we found it, didn't think. Anyway too late now. Just waiting to hear what's going on. Bricking it when the news comes on. Haven't told anyone, have you? I'll let you know as soon as.

Say *what*? All I knew was that Cindy did a runner after the whole Holly-swallowed-ecstasy thing because she thought Holly was going to be taken into care. But what's all *this* about?

To: Ben
From: Cindy
Subject: That night

No, of course I haven't told anyone. If there was no one there, it couldn't have been as bad as we thought. At least Holly is safe now. Jude has a beautiful place here, right by the sea, and she's going to take care of everything. If you go round all nervous, people are going to know there's something up. Please calm down Ben, it was an accident and it's over with.
Cind

To: Cindy
From: Ben
Subject: Re: That night

It was Anna Green. They found her today, unconscious. She's come round and it's mainly cuts and bruises. Dad and all the police are swarming round doing witness appeals and it's been on the local news. Went to the hospital to see Anna. Nightmare. Everyone was gathered round her telling her they'd find the hit-and-run driver. Can't concentrate on anything. Don't know what I should do.

To: Ben
From: Cindy
Subject: Re: That night

Oh God, I can't believe this. Don't do anything or say anything. I really like Anna, I worked with her in Dad's shop a few times. Is she honestly OK? You have to tell me the truth. But listen, Ben, dropping ourselves in it isn't going to help her. You always hear about things like this going unsolved. There's nothing we can do, so don't start panicking, OK?

To: Cindy
From: Ben
Subject: Re: That night

The police have got Tony in for questioning. They've found some damage on the front of his car. Plus, loads of witnesses saw Tony off his face at the Dog earlier that night, so how did his car turn up back outside his house if he didn't drive drunk? I've stitched him up. Dad reckons they're all convinced he's guilty and they're going to keep taking him in till he coughs for it. The students are out for his blood. Haven't slept for two days thinking about it. Can't let him go down for something he hasn't done.

To: Ben
From: Cindy
Subject: Re: That night

What am I supposed to do, give myself up so Holly loses her mum, and Dad has to watch me being carted off to jail? I'm sorry Ben, I know this sounds selfish, but my family is all I've got. Tony could get off anyway. Dad's turned up. I'm 'making a coffee' for him right now while he's talking to Jude, so got to be quick. I've got to tell him that I'm not going back, that's going to break his heart, so no way can I tell him about Anna as well. When he walked in with his little overnight bag I nearly cried, he looked so tired and relieved to see me. I love him so much, but me and Jude have given him nothing but grief. Please be careful what you say, for Holly's sake. I mean it Ben. Keep it together and don't do anything stupid.
Got to go
Cindy

I feel giddy. There's way too much information here, too much buried stuff that means too much to too many people close to me. Can't handle this.

3 May 2001   5:45am

So much for sleep.

> To: Cindy
> From: Ben
> Subject: Tony
>
> I've told Dad. I couldn't stand keeping quiet any more. Don't worry, I told him I was driving. He said more or less the same as you – keep your head down and say nothing, even though he knows Tony is still in the frame (what a great policeman). I felt like I had to go along with it. I don't know. Still really unhappy about it.

> To: Ben
> From: Cindy
> Subject: Re: Tony
>
> *You're* unhappy?? What the hell did you do that for? So you said you were driving, big deal, do you expect me to be grateful or something? I can't believe you put me and Holly at risk just because you were on a guilt trip. What if your dad changes his mind? What do I do, sit and wait for a knock on the door? I thought you understood how much Holly means to me, but I was so wrong. Thanks for nothing. Don't contact me again.

OK, so it all happened a while ago, but everyone knows how badly Anna's been affected by the hit-and-run. She's always said the worst part of her ordeal was not knowing who was responsible. Now I've got the power to set her mind at rest. But at what cost?

I throw the yo-yo around for a bit, then poke around in the remains of my instant noodles for the least rubbery one in the pot. I stand at the window and look out at the empty street.

You go digging through people's private affairs, you're going to find things you don't want to hear. But now I *do* know – what? I've always reckoned that Ben is too smarmy for his own good – I couldn't help taking Luke's side over the Mandy thing – but there's no way I'm going to put Cindy in jeopardy. I'm going to file this one away for later. You never know, it could be useful if I ever happen to need a favour from Fireman Sam.

It'd be another story if Tony ever found out the truth, not that I ever intend to help him. I wonder what secrets his e-mails must hold. He spends so much time minding everyone else's business that there must be some real gems in there. I've been trying to crack his password for weeks. I have another go.

masterchef	Please re-enter password
ihatefinn	Please re-enter password
ihatestudents	Please re-enter password
landlord	Please re-enter password
annoyingcontrolfreak	Please re-enter password

In his typical, Tony-esque style, he's chosen something totally impenetrable and highly effective in keeping out the likes of me. How is it that he can even make something like choosing a password completely irritating? I can almost see his smug little face grinning at me every time I get it wrong. I start to open O.B.'s account. I think I've earned some light relief.

Someone outside the door. Hold that thought.

7 May 2001   1:45am

I find these among Lewis's mail, all dated yesterday.

To:	Finn
From:	Lewis
Subject:	My travels

I know, I know. I'm sorry I've been out of the game so long. I just need a few more days to tie up some loose ends. It's been brilliant, getting out, meeting people. I've been so caught up in running the club I've forgotten what business is all about. Anyway, I got chatting to this old fella when I was on the Guinness and he told me about his neighbour who'd just died. I went round to this cottage and it was full of really classic, Irish stuff – pottery, furniture, the lot. I've offered two grand and the widow's thinking about it. If we get it, it'll be snapped up the minute it hits the yard. I knew there was a reason I've been feeling lucky.

Lewis

To: Lewis
From: Mandy
Subject: Where are you?

I thought you were going to ring last night? I tried to call you at your bed and breakfast but they said you'd moved on to some posh-sounding hotel. Anyway, I called reception there but they had no booking under your name. I rang the B&B back, but they said you'd definitely gone there. Is everything OK?

Mandy

To: Mandy
From: Lewis
Subject: Re: Where are you?

Sorry about that. Yeah, the hotel turned out to be full so I stayed somewhere else. Work stuff has been really full-on this last couple of weeks. I know I said I'd ring you yesterday, but I was trying to tie up a deal – sorry.

How is Mum? She seemed a bit stressed when I left. I think she's feeling the strain of dealing with work and Tom. Pass on my love.

See you soon

Lewis

What's wrong with this picture? Since when does anyone leave a bed and breakfast without making sure the next place has a free room? Unless Lewis left the first place as himself, then checked into the hotel as Kurt Benson. Far-fetched? OK, maybe. More so than carrying around Kurt's driving licence? I don't think so.

Still, I can't help feeling like I'm getting carried away with myself. In this mood, I could read Anna Green's e-mails and suspect her of sleeping her way round half the men in Chester. I decide to pick up where I was interrupted the other night and enter O.B.'s e-mail. I worked out the password – *caprice* – after hearing O.B. discuss his fantasies with Max. There's no reaction from O.B. to the less-than-flattering Izzy e-mail I passed on, but then he'd hardly boast about it, would he?

To: O.B.
From: Max
Subject: Twenty questions

Know you're busy mate, what with your busy schedule of morning telly and afternoon telly, so I did the honours.

What time is it?	4:15pm (waking up time)
Name as it appears on your birth certificate:	Samuel Timothy Sebastian O'Brien
Nickname at school:	O.B., Zit
Pets:	Trouser snake – 'Tiny'
Piercings:	See above. Like a Slinky, mate
Tattoos:	'My girlfriend' on right palm
Been to how many continents?	Three, including Blackpool
Dumper or dumpee?	Dumped on
Favourite place* to be kissed:	Back of kebab van when she's had fifteen pints (*only place)
Talker or listener?	'Ey?
Most annoying trait in others:	They won't sleep with me

Fantasy partner:	Anyone who doesn't need a foot-pump
Most embarrassing incident:	So many to choose from, so little time
Fighter or lover?	Either way I might sprain my wrist
Favourite position:	Attached to lady
Proudest moment:	Losing cherry
Favourite word:	*Please*?
Biggest fear:	Cherry growing back
Loved somebody so much it made you cry?	Yes
If yes, who?	Palmela Handerson

I head for a swarm of e-mails sent and received on the same day – usually a good sign that there's something worth knowing about.

To: O.B.
From: Max
Subject: Tomorrow

All right mate
You up for a few bevvies after you finish lectures?
Max

To: Max
From: O.B.
Subject: Re: Tomorrow

Sorry, got to give it a swerve. Essay crisis.

To: Jonno, Marley, Paul, Jez, Josh, Sprout, Wilco
From: O.B.
Subject: Operation Get Stubbsy Pissed

OK men, here's the plan… Straight to the Dog after lectures, few pints before he arrives, then we prepare the birthday cocktail. Word of warning – the landlord gets arsy about drinking games but, if we buy one of every short behind the bar and tip it all into a pint glass or two, he won't notice the difference. Stock up on beer tokens and

remember – trips to the cashpoint and/or bog will be deducted from overall scores (worst luck Marley, AKA hamster bladder!!).
May the force be with you.
Sam

To: O.B.
From: Max
Subject: Re: Tomorrow

Is that student code for bird?
Max

To: Max
From: O.B.
Subject: Re: Tomorrow

No.

To: O.B.
From: Max
Subject: Re: Tomorrow

Thought not you palm pilot. By the way, what have you done to Chloe? I saw her giving you big time dirties outside the canteen this afternoon.
Max

To: O.B.
From: Chloe
Subject: Max

Essay crisis? Can't your powers of deception come up with anything better than that? Yes, as you've probably guessed, I spoke to Max today. I think you're being so tight to him. The whole college knows where you're going tomorrow. What have you got to lose by inviting him along? Apart from my opinion of you as a snobby, hypocritical, little worm. Oh, and did I mention hypocritical? cos you don't mind going round to his house for Playstation 2 sessions, but heaven forbid you should be seen in public with someone who works for a living.

I'm aware this is technically none of my business, but there was a time when the three of us used to be mates. I don't find it as easy to forget as you seem to.

Give him a break. What are you so afraid of?

Chloe

No reply from O.B., unsurprisingly. I feel like Max is getting a raw deal. I search through for something embarrassing I can send him to even things out a bit. Ah, I wonder if Max has seen this? Trust O.B. to try and grab the writer/producer credit.

To: Maverick Recording Company
From: O.B.
Subject: Our demo

I am writing to ask whether you have any feedback on our demo, 'Get Down With That Thing' by {insert name – see Max}, which we sent to you some weeks ago, and which is currently causing a big stir on the club scene in the northwest of England.

I know that, as head of the label, Madonna is very committed to capturing the new sounds of the street. Our music reflects the daily struggle to strive and survive in the harsh, urban environment where we were born and raised. The track was written and produced by me, with some sampling done by Max Cunningham.

If you have decided that {insert name} is not right for you at this time, could you please use our return postage to forward our CD to Guy Ritchie's office, as we feel our distinctive music is a film soundtrack waiting to happen.

Yours keeping it real
Sam O'Brien

Before I log off (my eyes *really* hurt), I see the 'Rules of the Stag' e-mail that came from Max. Every time I come across this, I'm convinced it'll contain some bit of information that will explain what's going on in Lewis's head. Apart from that, I'm burning up with sheer curiosity. I try some passwords to open the encrypted files. Nothing. Then I try a few more. I keep trying and, before I know it, there goes an hour. But tomorrow I have to be up and doing

normal person stuff just like everyone else. Better not push my luck.
I'm out of here.

10 May 2001   1:15am

I overheard Ruth and Geri talking outside Deva today. I couldn't stop
for a full-on earwig, but I got the impression that Ruth has been
dropping round to the Loft for cosy chats with Finn (subject: three
guesses) and that this has 'really helped'. Maybe it's all quite
innocent, but if anyone's got a nose for scandal, it's Geri.

To: Anna
From: Geri
Subject: Kittens

I'm in the media lab. Adam and Izzy have just left. Adam took a
one-second break from finding her wonderful to talk to me about
his film project. I psyched myself up to act normal with him, but
then suddenly I'm avoiding eye contact like I'm twelve and it's my
first crush. And all the time the Ice Queen is stood behind him
giving me frosties. I know why I feel like this. Last night I did a
really stupid thing. I slept in a shirt he left over at the house a few
weeks ago. How sad and girly is that? Make sure I burn it will
you?

      Anyway, just remembered last night's dream – can you look it
up in your book? (Sorry, I know this is all a bit Sabrina.) I was in bed
and there were loads of kittens coming through the door and
jumping onto the duvet. Please let it be something good.
Geri

To: Geri
From: Anna
Subject: Re: Kittens

Got an Izzy-ism for the list – 'Why don't you ever buy decent food
instead of all this cheap stuff?' (To Alex, this morning)
      There's no point me saying you have to get over him, is there?

Kittens are supposed to mean 'a short-lived but enjoyable affair is
on its way.' Sounds like you'd better buy a litter tray.
Anna

To: Anna
From: Geri
Subject: Swimming pool

Just heard Adam and Izzy giggling in the lunch queue. Turns out
they bribed Matt to let them have keys to the swimming pool, and
they ended up having a skinny dip at 1.30 this morning. OK, I know
you're thinking so what. It's just that me and Adam did exactly the
same thing when we were together. I don't know why, but this hurts
me more than anything else they've done. Seems like Izzy isn't
content with taking Adam, she wants to take my memories as well.
(Oh God, drama queen alert! But that's how it feels.)
Geri

To: Geri
From: Anna
Subject: Re: Swimming pool

Perhaps Adam was the one trying to relive his memories.
Anna

To: Anna
From: Geri
Subject: Re: Swimming pool

Thanks Anna, you always say the right thing. Don't think I believe it
though. (It seems Izzy was up for a third time but Adam suffered
shrinkage due to the cold, in case you were wondering.)
Geri

I can't help myself – I *have* to send Geri's first 'Swimming pool'
message to Izzy. It's slightly risky but I'm getting restless. Just to add
an extra bit of spice, I make it look as though it's been sent from
Adam's account.

To: Geri
From: Anna
Subject: (No subject)

I don't want you to think this has all blown over just because you've
moved out. What you've done is just sinking in. Did you honestly
think we'd be OK with the fact that hidden cameras were recording
everything we did and said?

    What sickens me most of all is the time you spent crying on my
shoulder about wanting to be with Adam, when all the time you
were conspiring with him against the rest of us. You whined about
him letting you down, but what you've done to us is far worse. Find
a dictionary and look up self-respect. Once you understand what it
means, you can start working out how to get some.
Anna

To: Anna
From: Geri
Subject: Sorry

Anna, I tried to talk to you in college today. I understand why you
avoided me when I saw you by the lockers. I'd have done the same.
I'm just going to tell you what happened, not because I'm trying to
excuse myself, but because you deserve to know. I found out about
the cameras and started setting up situations to tease Adam. He
saw what I was doing and confronted me about it. I should have
told him I was going to blow the game to everyone in the house. But
he was terrified he'd lose his project, so I agreed to carry on.

    I feel like I sold out my friends just to get in with Adam again,
and I'm so ashamed. Most of all I regret hurting you. Please can we
talk?
Geri

To: Geri
From: Anna
Subject: Re: Sorry

Crap, Geri. All you're saying is that you tried to score points over
Izzy by sharing a secret with Adam. I always knew you were
obsessed with him, but I never thought you'd dump on your

friends. OK, so he's split with Izzy, but what have you got out of it? Has he got back together with you? Does he respect you more? I doubt it somehow. I can't believe you used to be someone I liked and trusted.
Anna

To: Jacqui
From: Geri
Subject: Hi Mum

Hi
Haven't heard from you for weeks so I assume you're OK. I never thought I'd say this, but here goes. Mum, I really need to see you. If there's any chance at all of you coming over just for a few days – I'm staying at Ruth's flat and I'm sure she wouldn't mind – I'd be really grateful. It's nothing major, I could just do with someone to talk to. Hope to hear from you soon.
Geri

To: Geri
From: Jacqui
Subject: Re: Hi Mum

Tell me you're not still mooning over Adam Morgan! Babe, Demetrius and I are flying to the Seychelles tonight (going for Brazilian wax in half an hour – pray for your old mum, sweetheart!) Go and punish the shops (tell your father I said so if he starts moaning).
Love and hugs
Mum

I call up the log-in page for Adam's mail server, studentmail.com, and type in his user name, adammorgan200.

gerihudson	Password not recognised
izzycornwell	Password not recognised
spielbergwannabe	Password not recognised
documentary	Password not recognised

I dredge my memory. Who was that backpacker who used to hang around Deva?

Can't remember her name.

jenny	Password not recognised
aussiechick	Password not recognised
australia	Password accepted

Cool. First thing I notice is there aren't that many e-mails in his files. He's obviously been through deleting stuff he doesn't want hanging around. That's total Adam, though – laid-back on the surface, pretty calculating underneath.

To: Adam
From: Kerri
Subject: Read this and weep

OK, picture a white sandy beach, blue water, palm trees, the works. You picturing? Then stick yours truly at the beach bar with a lap-top. I'm on the coast of Thailand in a place that's more *The Beach* than *The Beach*. Hate to make you chunder, Mr Tipp-Ex, but I'm tanned, chilled and having the time of my life. I tried really hard to be a regular nine-to-fiver but only served three months inside a maximum-security facility, otherwise known as a call-centre. I hooked up with another inmate (female, since you ask) and we decided to do Southeast Asia (again), then on to – who knows? So what's going on with these two pieces of blonde totty? So let's recap, they're both rich, but one's snooty with it, right? You left Number One, were thinking of going back to her, met Number Two instead, but deep down you think you may still have the roaring hots for Number One, right? Well, I suppose you've got to imagine some excitement now you've settled for pipe, slippers and hot, buttered crumpet (as opposed to a cool, toned and – if I say so myself – pretty perky-looking one). Ah, well… The offer, as always, is open… Want to catch up with us in Europe?
Kerri

To: Kerri
From: Adam
Subject: Re: Read this and weep

Yeah, cheers for rubbing it in. There's trouble kicking off like you wouldn't believe. I've been doing this film project that's a bit too controversial for the people here to get their heads round. As for my private life, don't even go there. Both 'Number One' and 'Number Two', as you put it, are finding me less than irresistible as a result of my project. Probably made a huge mistake getting involved with English women in the first place. I'm fed up with battles of wills and mind games. Why didn't you just get a cattle prod and force me onto the plane last time?
Adam

To: Adam
From: Kerri
Subject: Re: Read this and weep

You mean 'huge mistake' messing her around/trapping off with her best mate/posting artistic pics of her on the net/proposing unnatural acts/doing whatever made them dump you?
Kerri
PS I think you only told yourself you still liked Number One as a defence against possible rejection by Miss Two. I think you're sold on this 'ice maiden' creature. I know you *so* well, Adam Morgan.

To: Kerri
From: Adam
Subject: Re: Read this and weep

Maybe. The whole thing's too weird to go into.
Adam

To: Adam
From: Kerri
Subject: Re: Read this and weep

Whatever. You are so not over Miss Two. Now, let me put this grubby triangle aside and turn my attention back to my earthly paradise. See you!
Kerri

To: Luke
From: Adam
Subject: Izzy

Saw you and Mandy in town with Izzy and that lot at lunchtime – did she say anything about me? No messing around.
Ad

To: Adam
From: Luke
Subject: Re: Izzy

You sad man. Face it, you're dead meat.
Luke

To: Izzy
From: Adam
Subject: Apologies

Iz, please answer your phone so we can talk about all this. I've made a huge balls-up and I'm really sorry. I started out with an idea that I thought was good but I didn't realise how much it'd end up affecting you. I should've kept you in the picture all along. Geri got involved by accident, and I wish she hadn't because I think it's made everything a lot more difficult. None of this was her fault. I put pressure on her to keep quiet because I didn't want the whole project to collapse. Now it looks as though I needn't have bothered, because it doesn't look like John Stuart is going to accept such an 'unethical' piece of work. I suppose I had this coming.

I know I'm a huge walking turd and I've got a massive amount of grovelling to do, but I can't start until you let me speak to you.
Adam

To: Adam
From: Izzy
Subject: Re: Apologies

You really don't need to start brushing up your grovelling technique because I haven't got the slightest bit of interest in what you have to say. I think your actions speak for themselves, don't you?
Don't give me the 'I had this coming' line – I know for a fact that you've got Ruth trying to fight your case with the college. It's so typical of you to reach for the fake humility when it suits you.
Geri's involvement is of no concern to me. But, for the record, she does have a mind of her own and should have thought twice before conspiring against her housemates. Not that her behaviour surprises me. We've always known exactly where her loyalty lies. Well, now you're free to take full advantage of it. You got the turd bit right. You two were made for each other.
Izzy

To: Izzy
From: Adam
Subject: Re: Apologies

You're making this out to be about me and Geri, and it so isn't. There's nothing between us and there's not going to be, ever. All she got out of it was the satisfaction of knowing what was going on when everyone else didn't. You know what she's like for winding people up. Please don't let this mess things up for us. We really need to talk.
Adam

To: Geri
From: Adam
Subject: Cameras

I know you're getting stick for the camera thing and I'm sorry. But it's too late to try and win people round again by slagging me off. I think you'd get a lot more respect if you defended the project. At least people would think you've got the guts to stand up for what we did.
Adam

To: Adam
From: Geri
Subject: Not me

I think it takes more guts to admit I was wrong. I realise this isn't
something you'll ever be capable of.
Geri

Before I've had a chance to think about it, I send Adam's 'Re:
Apologies' e-mail to Geri – the one about there being 'nothing
between us... ever'. It might be just what she needs to put her out of
her misery. Once I've sent it, I feel a bit scared. It's probably just my
imagination, but I feel like I got evils from Izzy this morning. But
then, who doesn't? And if she really suspected, she'd be doing a lot
more than giving me funny looks outside Drive 'n' Buy. I'm going to
have to develop a thicker skin. Time to disappear.

11 May 2001   2:17am

Didn't get much sleep last night. I woke up around 5am, gasping like
I was just seconds away from drowning. I'd had this dream where I
was being chased through the streets by Izzy, Geri, Finn, Adam and
Ruth. They were yelling and swearing and chucking things at me. I
was running as fast as I could, but I had these metal brace-type
things on my legs like Forrest Gump. They trapped me and forced
me into the college driveway and suddenly I was face-to-face with
Lewis, who turned a huge water cannon on me and blasted me back
towards the mob. That's when I jolted myself awake, soaked in
sweat. Don't think I need Anna's book to work out what this means.

To: Geri, Adam
From: Izzy
Subject: Re: Swimming pool

Why have I suddenly received an e-mail from Geri to Anna, via Adam's
e-mail address? If it's supposed to be a joke, it's incredibly sad.

To: Adam, Izzy
From: Geri
Subject: Re: Apologies

Oh, please. This was supposed to achieve *what*, exactly? I don't know which of you had the brilliant idea to send me this but, if either of you is so insecure that you have to 'remind' me that I'm no longer seeing Adam, I really pity you. Has it occurred to you that this e-mail is almost two months old? Some of us have moved on. Geri

To: Izzy
From: Geri
Subject: Re: Swimming pool

What are you on about?

To: Geri, Adam
From: Izzy
Subject: Re: Swimming pool

See attachment.
(Attachment: Swimming pool)

To: Izzy
From: Adam
Subject: Re: Swimming pool

This has nothing to do with me. Where did it come from?

To: Adam
From: Izzy
Subject: Re: Swimming pool

Your e-mail address! Adam, did you honestly not send it? Because if you didn't, something's going on.

Uh-oh. This doesn't look good. Have I overstepped the mark? Don't know. I'm not scared, just exhilarated. I've never felt my heart beating in the back of my throat before.

To: Anna
From: Geri
Subject: Hello

Well, we managed to have a semi-conversation yesterday. OK, so it was only 'have you got change for the machine?' but it was a start. I understand if you don't want to be my friend, but it makes things easier if we can at least get on.

I got this weird e-mail yesterday that I can't get out of my mind. It was Adam to Izzy, just after everyone found out about the hidden camera thing. Anyway, he was telling her that there was nothing going on between me and him, and there never would be. My first thought was that Izzy is preparing to have him back. But then I noticed it came from him. Don't know what he was trying to tell me by sending me this, but I'm glad he did. There's something about seeing him grovel that makes him seem sort of smaller (in every way) than I've always thought he was. Perhaps this is the big Santa-doesn't-exist moment that I've needed.

My other news is I've been 'seeing' Taylor. Only Ruth knows so far and I hope she's not going to blab. Not that it's a big secret, but the minute it becomes public you're a couple and that's *so* not what either of us are up for at the moment.

Anyway, I don't know if you'll want to reply to this. I *do* know there's no one else I could really tell. I'm not asking for violins because I know it's my fault. But if you did decide to reply, you'd make my day (I know, how sad is that?).
Geri
PS Chloe tells me you and Alex are back 'on.' If that's what you want, good for you. Really trying not to nag, but be careful, Anna.
PPS Dreamt of going up a staircase that kept getting narrower and steeper until there was no handrail, and then I fell. Any chance of hearing what your book says?

To: Geri
From: Anna
Subject: Re: Hello

Don't worry, of course Alex and I are being careful. We check each room for cameras before we do it.

Anna
PS I'm sure you can spare £5.99 for your own copy.

To: Geri
From: Triple X Adult Fantasy Club
Subject: Welcome!!

Congratulations!! You have been recommended as a new customer by Mr Adam Morgan of Chester, England. Please choose your free introductory gift from our range of adult pleasure toys!! As a member of our Gold Priority VIP Club you enjoy an automatic 10% discount on all latex wear!!

To: Adam
From: Geri
Subject: So not funny

You've cost me my home and my friends with your stupid project, now I receive this. If it happens again, you'll be walking around with an 'adult pleasure toy' inserted somewhere less than pleasurable.
Geri
(Attachment: Welcome!!)

To: Geri
From: Adam
Subject: Not me

This wasn't me, I swear.

To: Izzy, Alex, Chloe, Matt, Anna, Ruth, O.B., Taylor, Finn, Adam
From: Geri
Subject: Weird e-mails

Is anyone else receiving misdirected e-mails or dodgy junk from mailing lists, supposedly from people they know?
Geri

Now I'm scared.

To: Geri
From: Izzy
Subject: Re: Weird e-mails

A couple of times, yeah. What's going on?

To: Izzy
From: Geri
Subject: Re: Weird e-mails

Duh! That's what I'm trying to find out. Do you think it could be Tony?

To: Geri, Izzy
From: Adam
Subject: Re: Weird e-mails

I think I've sussed who's doing it.

To: Adam
From: Izzy
Subject: Re: Weird e-mails

Who?? It's Tony, isn't it?

To: Adam
From: Geri
Subject: Re: Weird e-mails

Well? Who is it?

To: Izzy, Geri
From: Adam
Subject: Re: Weird e-mails

Don't worry. I've got it sorted.

As I read this, my net provider crashes and the phone cuts in. My heart slams against my ribs. It has to be Adam. I'm finished.

Someone's answered it. I can hear talking, then some laughter. I try to calm myself but my nerve's gone for tonight. Adam's sussed me, I can feel it.

12 May 2001   12:35am

Spent the whole day in fear of Adam confronting me. I tried to work out what I'd say, but I didn't get very far. What excuse could I possibly have? I check Adam's e-mail. I'm pretty certain my luck's run out.

> **Password not recognised**

I try Izzy's, then Geri's, then O.B.'s. Same story. They've changed their passwords as a result of the panic Geri's caused. Yeah, well I didn't get this far without knowing a thing or two about what makes them tick. I'll be back.

12 May 2001   1:25am

Cracked them all – and in less than an hour! God, how stupid do they think I am – did they really believe they could stop me by a simple change of password? A few months ago, this might have been a problem, but now I know enough about them to get into their heads as and when I like – and they can't do a thing about it. I've got to be a bit more stealthy, though. Can't risk Lewis changing his password and coming up with one that really is secure, that'd be a disaster. I've had my fun. It's time to get serious.

> To: Adam
> From: Izzy
> Subject: Re: Weird e-mails
>
> Well? Who was it??

> To: Adam
> From: Geri
> Subject: Re: Weird e-mails
>
> Still no explanation? Admit it, it was you.

To: Zara
From: Adam
Subject: You're dead

Very clever – but not clever enough. Who's immature enough to sign Geri up for sex toy catalogues and to misdirect old e-mails? Duh, let me think. You're so dead next time I see you.
Adam

To: Adam
From: Zara
Subject: Re: You're dead

Bothered! OK, I did the pervy one, but what are you on about misdirecting e-mails?

To: Zara
From: Adam
Subject: Re: You're dead

Zara, when you've been caught red-handed you stop arguing, OK?

To: Adam
From: Zara
Subject: Re: You're dead

But I really didn't!! You're off your head!!

Can't believe it, *I'm safe*.

Better catch up with Lewis. He's only sent one new e-mail in the past week. I'm so keen to read it I find myself swearing at the computer in the moment it takes for the message to open.

To: Dennis Richardson, c/o HMP Blackwood
From: Lewis
Subject: (No subject)

I've been on my own a lot lately and I've had a lot of time to think (not as much as you, I admit). I now know why I did the thing that reminded me of you. I've never been into religion but I think someone – something, whatever – was testing me. There was a

flash of you in me for a few seconds and the test was whether I
would recognise it. And I did, straight away, which means it can't
happen again. So we're not alike at all. In fact, I'd say we're
opposites.

You tried really hard to ruin your family's lives but you know
what, Dad, you've failed so badly. Mandy's stronger and more
confident than she's ever been. Mum's with someone who loves
her and makes her happy, and Tom has given her loads of new
energy. And guess what, my life's in pretty good shape too. How's
yours?
Lewis

I get up and open the window. I get this dizzy, sick feeling, like
being in a rollercoaster car that's been pulled right to the top of the
track. I knew he hated his dad, but it's still a shock to feel the full
force of it. Still no reply. Lewis might as well have written a letter
and torn it up. But maybe that's the point. It's obvious he's trying
to convince himself of something, I just don't know what, and I
don't think I've ever been so desperate to find out. Aargh
FRUSTRATION!!!

I log off from Lewis's server and sign myself into Finn's. I
overheard him and Mandy today. She was asking him if there was
any news from Lewis and Finn was trying to make out he wasn't
expecting any, in his typical, unruffled way. I couldn't work out
whether he was genuinely cool about it or if he was trying not to
worry her. I find a message that's a couple of days old.

To: Finn
From: Ruth
Subject: My head hurts

I hate you. Got 15 mins to prepare a lecture and my brain feels like
it's come loose from its stump. What did you do to me? Hope you
feel at least 10x as crap as I do.
Ruth

To: Ruth
From: Finn
Subject: Re: My head hurts

Don't know what you're talking about. I wasn't drunk. I was just
walking around in very big shoes. OK, school night and everything,
it was a bit naughty. But come on, we put the world to rights* didn't
we? All I can say is thank you my darling Vicky for letting me have a
bed on the barge.
Finn
*i.e. both admitted that we worry about Lewis 24/7, even though he
can't be arsed to let us know where/when/how we're ever going to
see him again.

To: Finn
From: Ruth
Subject: Re: My head hurts

Head now hurts less. Had lunch and lecture nightmare is now
over. Have to admit last night was one of the best for ages (except
that totally unnecessary 'Man! I Feel Like a Woman!' incident),
mainly because we didn't plan it. Yes, I know Lewis kind of
dominated things, but I'm glad in a way. I feel a lot clearer in my
mind about him now. When (if?) he comes back, I'm going to be a
lot more relaxed about things. You're right, he is at his worst
when he thinks people are waiting for him to mess things up.
Sounds simple now, but I couldn't have worked it out myself. Do it
again sometime?
Ruth

To: Ruth
From: Finn
Subject: Re: My head hurts

I owed you one for convincing me to move to the flat and advising
me on the whole baby thing. Perhaps you can help me with another
dilemma. I want to buy Vicky something for the flat to say a bit of a
sorry for last night (I forgot to phone her…). What do you think
about one of those you've-woken-up-and-hey-presto-there's-a-

cup-of-tea things? I've got the catalogue here. And is cream better,
or white? Discuss. Please.
Finn

To: Finn
From: Ruth
Subject: Re: My head hurts

I'd go for white, but are you sure she wants one? No offence, but
aren't they a bit old-persony? Think about the sort of thing she
likes.
Ruth

To: Ruth
From: Finn
Subject: Re: My head hurts

It's not what *I* think she'd like that matters, is it?
Finn

To: Finn
From: Ruth
Subject: Re: My head hurts

It's totally what you think she'd like. You're her husband, she'd like
whatever you get her. Why don't you trust your own instincts for
once? (I'll bet you'll go for the tea thing now.)
Ruth

To: Finn
From: Carol
Subject: Your new home

Hello Mister
It's 8:05pm. We've just left Port of Spain, Trinidad, en route for
Miami (eventually). I'm on deck with a laptop I've borrowed off a
very friendly diamond dealer and am looking out over a sunset that
makes me want to cry, it's so lush.

Enough of my ship — Tony tells me you've abandoned yours. Is
he winding me up, or what? He says you're installed in domestic
bliss in a two-bedroom flat over the other side of Hollyoaks.

complete with toasted sandwich maker. Well, I never thought I'd see the day. Did you get tired of sticking two fingers up at convention, or has Mrs Finn smoothed off some of your famous edge?

Maybe I'll drop by one day when I'm visiting Mum and Dad.
Carol

To: Carol
From: Finn
Subject: Re: Your new home

We moved because Vicky hated the barge (almost as much as you did, if I remember rightly) and yes, thanks, I'm happier than I've ever been. As for losing my edge, there's nothing edgy about doing what everyone expects me to do, i.e. staying on the barge. I don't think there's anything cosy or conventional about doing exactly what I want. Which is to have a home that makes both of us happy. Which we are. And yes, we'd be delighted to show you round.
Finn

To: Finn
From: Carol
Subject: Re: Your new home

Root canal, big drill, whoops – did I hit a nerve? (Did I *say* 'cosy'?)
Carol

That's the last e-mail, but I can't let things lie. I send Lewis's e-mail to his dad to Finn. Just want to see how surprised he'll be and whether he'll give anything away. I just heard someone on the pavement outside. I'll have to call it a night. Don't want anyone wondering why my desk light is on.

13 May 2001   12:45am

To: Ruth
From: Finn
Subject: Strange

Alright Ruth?
Bit of a strange one, this. Got an e-mail from Lewis that was for his
dad. Of course, I did the decent thing and deleted it straight away.
Well, almost. The thing was, he was talking about how he did
something that reminded him of his dad. I know I shouldn't even be
discussing this. It's just I know all about his dad and this really
freaked me out. If he's in some kind of trouble I just want to help him.
Any ideas?

To: Finn
From: Ruth
Subject: Re: Strange

He probably means his gambling. His dad's an alcoholic, so maybe
he was talking about addiction. Weird how it ended up getting sent
to you, though.
PS Did you really delete it? If not, can I see it?

To: Ruth
From: Finn
Subject: Re: Strange

Never thought of that, but it makes sense now.
(Attachment: (No subject))

Not convinced by this explanation from Ruth, it's all too tidy. Not
convinced that she believes it, either. But the great thing is, Finn
doesn't seem to wonder how the message ended up in his inbox. I
think I've been over-cautious.

Carol's mention of Tony has made me more determined than ever
to crack the fortress that is his e-mail account. I spend half an hour

getting knocked back as I attempt to work out his password. It's so frustrating to know I've been outwitted by Tony Hutchinson of all people – half-man, half-apron.

I bring up Zara's log-in screen, expecting her to be an easy target. But after twenty minutes I'm stumped. I must be losing my touch. I try her friends, the ones who are always hanging around in Deva. I don't know much about them, but I figure that at least one of them will have picked something really obvious as a password. I strike lucky with Lisa – *lhunter* – and Steph – *slipknot*.

To:	Steph
From:	Abby
Subject:	Saturday

You want to go up town on Saturday? Zara said something about it ages ago in the two seconds she managed to peel herself off Brian. He's all she goes on about nowadays, she doesn't care about her m8s and she's got so boring. Must be sexual frustration because they still haven't done it. (Do you reckon he's gay?) I told her I was thinking of going in 2c those trousers I've got my eye on but she 'didn't hear' me. (Bothered!) If she's not going to make the effort, I'm not going to. Why don't we go just the two of us this week?
Ab

I send this to Zara. It could spare her a lot of future emotional trauma to find out what her friends really think of her. Yeah, right. If everyone read what other people are saying about them, would anyone have any friends left? I've certainly got a few scores to settle after reading things people have written about me.

To:	Steph
From:	Zara
Subject:	Help

God, I can't understand this molecule stuff, can't believe we've got to hand it in tomorrow morning! Have you done any of it yet? Got a thing about Slipknot for you out of *Heat*. Apparently they have this dead bird in a jar that they all get a whiff of before they go on stage so they can make themselves blow chunks. How gross is that?? Why don't they just get Miss Webb backstage and pay her to breathe her death breath on them??!

Help Steph, I've got to hand something in or Clarke is going to go postal.

Za

To: Zara
From: Steph
Subject: Re: Help

We can copy Lisa's, I bet she's done it, I knew she'd be useful for something! Shouldn't say that should I, cos I know you like her. Abby says you've got a stalker!

I think she's OK but I saw her going for chips with her dad just now, she had this pink, woolly top on, it was worse than sad. I feel a bit sorry for her. Maybe we can sort her out. Have you got any tokens left, cos 'Warning' by Green Day is wicked. Track three is about this boy asking a girl if she'll sleep with him if he promises to go to church with her... Remind you of anyone?? I'm only messing, but seriously, do you think you're ever going to get it on with Brian? Just asking cos Abby reckons it's your two-month anniversary – what did he get you?

Steph

To: Steph
From: Zara
Subject: Re: Help

Why do you keep asking, Steph? I know you've always fancied him, but get over it. Me and Brian are really happy and we don't need to jump into bed to prove it to anyone. Tell Abby it's her hundred-and-whatever month anniversary of being single (she is such a stirrer). By the way, I heard Dave Tickner telling that thin one in his Maths class that Rich Thomas really likes you. I think you should go for it, he's alright looking. You'd be loads happier if you had a boyfriend.

Za

I close Steph's account and open Lisa's. I've never even spoken to her. I don't know whether this should make me feel more guilty or less about ram-raiding her private thoughts. All I know is that I get the same old buzz seeing all her e-mails scrolling up in front of me.

To: Kim
From: Lisa
Subject: Welcome to paradise

You know how when you're dreading something, you tell yourself it can't really be that bad? Well, I lied. It's worse. I'm sitting in the 'computer suite' (it mings) at Hollyoaks Comprehensive with a spotty meathead looking over my shoulder, but he can just GET STUFFED if he thinks I'm going to log off just cos he's waiting. Can't believe I'm really here. Only met four people so far: Zara, Abby, Brian and some blonde (can't remember her name). Zara is a bit gobby and at first I wasn't sure about her, but it turns out she's OK. Brian is Mr Nice. Abby is your basic nightmare – a popular bitch. She tried to rip my blazer as some sort of now-you're-one-of-the-gang thing. (Excuse me, *how* old are you?)

The worst thing about Hollyoaks Comp. is it's different to Woodvale but exactly the same. Meathead Boy behind me is like Sean Saunders with bad hair. Abby is kind of Juliet Larson with smaller boobs and hair extensions. Brian is Michael Allen gone Goth. It's like I know them but they don't know me. There's something about this that's really depressing.

Anyway, to cut a tedious story short, I ended up in lunchtime detention, which turned out to be the best part of the day, cos I sort of started getting on with Zara. But surprise, surprise, I was all quiet and shy just like the bad old days at Woodvale. (I make myself sick.) Remember it took me months to get my confidence back after all the bad stuff happened? (Or began – it's not like it's over, is it?) Well, now I'm suddenly back to smiling and praying I don't offend anyone and trying to be invisible. I just feel like I haven't got enough energy left to start again and to try and be myself. (Like I can explain all this to Mum and Dad.)

Slap everyone round the face for me. Don't tell me what they're all up to cos I'll probably start blubbing and come across as even more of a sap than I have already.
Lisa

To: Dan
From: Lisa
Subject: First day

Just in case you were wondering how the New Girl's doing… It's sort of like Woodvale but sort of not. It more or less sucks, but there are one or two cool people here. Been to many lectures today? A reply would be good. (If I can get back on this lame computer to read it. You students are so cushy having access all day.)
Lisa

To: Lisa
From: Dan
Subject: Re: First day

I know it's a tough one, but you'd be better off making friends instead of reading this. The sooner you stand on your own two feet, the less it will suck. By the way, if Mum and Dad ask how your day went, you don't need to go into details. Just tell them it's going OK, blah blah, you made a few friends, etc., alright? (If you saw what Dad was like this morning you really don't need me telling you this, but just in case.)
Take care sis
Dan

With all this in mind, I flip back to Steph's e-mails. I want to find out whether she's realised there's more to Lisa than meets the eye.

To: Steph
From: Abby
Subject: Lisa

Oh my God, have I got goss… We were waiting to get into the disco when Lisa's brother turned up. He acted like he was her dad, telling

her he'd pick her up and to be a good girl, etc. Ben and Luke were on the door and they started fighting. Her brother came back and marched her off saying the club must be dodgy and she just went without saying anything, she didn't even argue with him! I knew she was a bit of a freak, but this was just weird. She must be really scared of him or something. (Have you ever seen him, by the way? How come such a spod has got such a fit brother??)
Ab

To: Zara
From: Steph
Subject: Lisa

Just heard what happened at the Loft, must have been soooo embarrassing for you, so glad I didn't go!! Can't believe she just walked off, I'd have gone mental if I was her. I knew she was a wimp, but can't she even stand up to her own brother? Have you talked to her since? What did she say – is she really ashamed?
Steph
PS Abby really fancies Lisa's brother, what's he like?

To: Steph
From: Zara
Subject: Re: Lisa

I can't believe it either. She needs some lessons in how to deal with her brother. I'd have given Luke a smack in the face if he'd tried that with me. She didn't even tell us what was going on, she just said 'I've got to go' and that was it. But then she got into Dan's car and it looked like she was crying. Don't tease her about it Steph, cos she was really upset.
Za
PS Yeah, he is fit, but not the type I go for.

I go back to Lisa's e-mail. I want to find out what really went on.

To: Lisa
From: Zara
Subject: (No subject)

What was all that about? Why did you leave? Me and Abby had an OK time but all through it I was wondering about you. You were looking forward to this for days, how come you let Dan make you go home? You could have told me he was going to try something like that and I'd have stood up for you.

If you let people walk all over you, they will – look at how Abby treats you. You're a Year 10 now and you should be able to do whatever you want. I'm not being a bitch, Lisa, I'm just telling you this for your own good. I don't want you to have a crap time at school because I think you're alright.

Za

To: Dan
From: Lisa
Subject: Last night

Yes, I know you've told me not to e-mail you from school but don't worry, I'm not wasting opportunities to make friends. There's not much chance of that after last night. And it looks like I'm going to lose the friends I've got. I've just had Abby sniggering at me all morning, telling everyone who'll listen about how I was dragged away from the Loft and asking me why I'm so 'scared' of my brother... What am I supposed to say? Don't blame Dad because he didn't make you do it. Why don't you think about what you're doing next time? (Not that there's going to be one – as if anyone's going to want to go anywhere with me after this.)

Lisa

To: Lisa
From: Dan
Subject: Re: Last night

I'm sorry you missed out on your night but I'm not going to apologise for what I did. OK, Dad didn't make me do it but, if he'd been there, he'd have done the same thing, you know he would. What if I let you go and something happened to you? Just think about it, Lisa. And don't go on about it in front of Mum and Dad tonight, alright?

Why don't you try and arrange a sleepover at Zara's or something?

Dan

To: Kim
From: Lisa
Subject: Re: Dancing queen

Well, my big night didn't quite go as planned. I was queuing to go in with Abby and Zara when Dan turned up to say he'd pick me up later. Then the two guys on security (Abby and Zara's brothers, would you believe) started scrapping. Dan saw them and decided the place was too dangerous for his precious little sister. Knew there was no point in arguing because he'd only come out with blah blah blah. But now everyone thinks I'm the biggest wuss on the planet because I'm 'afraid' to tell my own brother where to get off. Even Zara has given me an e-lecture about the importance of not being a wimp. I think she feels like she's taken a chance on me and I let her down (and in front of bitchface Abby herself). So I guess I've been given a warning. People are only going to give me so many chances before they get fed up with me. Somehow I'm going to have to find a way of playing the game. What's the alternative? Lunch on my own for the next two years? Mmm, *please*.
Lisa

I'm intrigued. I can't work out why Dan is so protective towards Lisa and why he's so afraid of rocking the boat with their parents. Who knows, maybe she *is* frightened of him. It seems like all her family wants to do is hush her up. Lisa's last e-mail was written just a few hours ago.

To: Zara
From: Lisa
Subject: Lunch

Maybe I'd better not sit on your table at lunch tomorrow. It's obvious that Abby really doesn't like me and she's been your friend a lot longer than I have. I just wanted to say that I'll understand if you're getting tired of all the hassle.
Lisa

As I'm reading this, I get the 'You Have Mail' icon. This has never happened to me before, at least not while I've been in someone else's inbox. I have a one-second debate with myself about whether it's ethical to open this before Lisa's had a chance to read it. I win.

To: Lisa
From: Zara
Subject: Re: Lunch

Abby may be my 'friend' but she's also a two-faced cow – see attachment. Like I didn't know that already. I bet she got Steph to send me this accidentally-on-purpose, but I'm not going to say anything cos I'm not giving them the satisfaction of thinking I'm bothered. You up for going into town yourself? I may be meeting Brian about five, but we won't throw the lips on each other in front of you, I promise (at least not while you're eating).
Za
(Attachment: Saturday)

I log off quickly, in case Lisa notices that she's got new mail and signs in to reply. I feel like I know her, even though she's just someone I've seen in Deva. I realise that I know more about her than her brother or parents ever will. None of the people who are closest to her seem to have any idea what really matters in her life. But maybe that's the way she likes it. I log back on. While I've been away she's written two new e-mails.

To: Zara
From: Lisa
Subject: Re: Lunch

Yeah, I think I'll be able to tear myself away from my crop rotation essay (ooh dilemma). Want to meet by the Clock about two?
Lisa

To: Kim
From: Lisa
Subject: Weird

Remember I told you about Zara, the OK one? I just got an e-mail from her. Steph (the blonde one) passed on an e-mail from Abby (the bitchy one) slagging Zara off and telling her not to ask her to go

to town on Saturday. And they're supposed to be her friends! That school is so twisted. I get the feeling no one really likes anyone else, they just pretend cos it makes them seem popular. How am I supposed to fit into all this? Like I know. I'm just going to keep my head down and watch my back.
Lisa

I don't believe in signs or omens or whatever, but I know this one's telling me it's time for bed.

14 May 2001   2:35am

Lewis is back. He arrived first thing this morning, all spiffed up in a straight-from-the-shop leather jacket that must have cost at least three hundred quid. Then he did a tour, going into Deva, Steam Team and the Dog to say hi and shake hands, every bit the long-lost son made good who's ridden into town to say the Milky Bars are on him. It made me think of the film *Swingers*, where all the guys go round reassuring each other that they look the business: *You're money, baby.* I don't know what I was expecting. Probably some tired, bitter man with the cares of the world on his shoulders. In fact, he didn't look much like the Lewis in my head at all, more like his more confident, more successful younger brother. Hard to believe it was the same person who sent those ranting messages to his dad. But maybe that's the point of all these new clothes.

I haven't heard or seen any evidence of Ruth today. Wonder if that's intentional? I check Finn's mail.

To: Finn
From: Ruth
Subject: Lewis

So he's back? Dad just rang me. How is he? Has he told you where he's been? I want to talk to him but I don't want it to seem like I've been lying in wait.
Ruth

To: Ruth
From: Finn
Subject: Re: Lewis

Your dad's right. He seems fine. Full of ideas about wanting to turn this place into the playground of the rich and loaded, and did I say rich? Yes, the theme seems to be let's chase the money and go upmarket. Don't know where all this is coming from, or where he's been apart from Ireland, but he's only ten feet away pulling himself a welcome-home shandy as I type. I'm glad to see him cos he's my mate and I've missed him, but I can see he's already starting to put Vic's back up.

I think what you're asking is whether he's mentioned you. And the answer is yes, kind of, but I have to leave the rest up to him. Why not come round?
Finn

To: Finn
From: Ruth
Subject: Re: Lewis

Not now. I need to psych myself up a bit first. I don't want to sound like a total girl, but what did he say about me?
Ruth

To: Ruth
From: Finn
Subject: Re: Lewis

Sorry, no can do. Just had one tiff already. He found out from his mum that I mentioned he had a gambling problem. I'm told I'm 'bang out of order.' I don't know, maybe I was wrong. I just want everything out in the open. Really don't want to get into the habit of distrusting him again.
Finn

I get the feeling that if Lewis knew they were tiptoeing around trying to read his moods, he'd blow a fuse. Especially now he's returned as the big man about town. He's got an image to protect, and it doesn't involve being monitored by his best mate and his ex.

I saw him with Max earlier today, throwing his money around in the Dog and being the ideal step-brother. I enter Max's account (password: *gisele*) and check out his latest mail.

To: Gayadvice
From: Max
Subject: My mate

Hello
I have a problem I hope you can help me with. I think a close friend of mine is having doubts about his sexuality. In fact, I think he may have made up his mind that he isn't the way I thought he was. He has always been straight (although hasn't had much luck) but has been spending a lot of time with a male friend. Today, I heard him tell his friend he loves him. I am very confused. What should I do?
Max

To: Max
From: Gayadvice
Subject: Re: My mate

Dear Max
The first thing to remember is you are not alone. We receive many requests for advice like yours. The biggest step to acceptance is total honesty – with yourself and with others. We've attached some advice sheets on coming out and dealing with a gay friend.

To: Gayadvice
From: Max
Subject: Re: My mate

Thanks for the advice. It really is for my mate, though, not me, his name's O.B. (Not that I'd be ashamed or anything if it was me.)
Max

This sounds like something to keep my eye on, but there's no mention of Lewis. While I'm in Max's mail, I notice that there's one of those Twenty questions things filled in by Tony.

What time it it?	1:15pm
Name as it appears on your birth certificate:	Anthony Hutchinson
Nickname at school:	Hutch, Rabbit, Starsky
Pets:	No (allergic)
Piercings:	No! (Where's that needle been?)
Tattoos:	Ditto
Been to how many continents?	Two
Dumper or dumpee?	I always dump a girl if she gets too 'dumpee'!
Favourite place to be kissed:	Four-poster bed
Talker or listener?	Listener, unless person is wrong
Most annoying trait in others:	Untidiness
Fantasy partner:	Hopefully she's not just a fantasy
Most embarrassing incident:	None; what doesn't kill you makes you stronger
Fighter or lover?	Lover
Favourite position:	Owner/manager (preferably of restaurant)
Proudest moment:	Opening student houses
Favourite word:	Organic
Biggest fear:	Not realising my potential
Loved somebody so much it made you cry?	Yes
If yes, who?	They know who they are

I *have* to get into his e-mails. No one is this boring naturally – it takes work. And a man who makes such a huge effort to sound bland must have a mental file bulging with unhealthy secrets. I've got to find it. Think.

catering	Password not recognised
ownermanager	Password not recognised
organic	Password not recognised

gourmet	Password not recognised

I pace around the room (very quietly) in total frustration and try a few more Tony-related words. Nothing. I log off and go to bed. I lie there restless with my mind in overdrive. *Think*. Who and what is Tony? What makes him tick?

I'm back at the computer. I've given up trying to sleep. I try words to do with Tony's mum (mrsfinnigan, theloft, ilovemum), his dad (accountant), his work (baconsarnie, caesarsalad, mrmorgan), his student houses (annagreen, chloebruce, cleaningrota), his obsessions (organicveg, makingmoney) and the totally Tony things he's been up to in the last few months (watersystem, christeningcake, godfather). All I can think of is that cake he made for Tom's christening, probably because I've got the late-night hunger again. Why is this so difficult?

icing	Password not recognised
marzipan	Password not recognised
pipingbag	Password not recognised
sugarcraft	Password accepted

It takes a second for this to sink in, then I spring up from my chair and do a (very quiet) dance around the room. I can't believe it. *Sugarcraft*. Such a Tony word for such a Tony thing. Why didn't I think of it sooner? Anyway, it doesn't matter now – it's showtime.

I sit back down and hunch up close to the screen. I want to read everything, right away, but it's impossible – there are hundreds of messages here. I whizz the mouse around the pad and click on one without looking.

To: Carol
From: Tony
Subject: Barcelona

It is 3:40am. Where are you? Mum got married today – sorry, yesterday. Been at the reception and ate and drank lots and very happy. Mum very happy and Finn too, he's not so bad after all. For every man there is one woman, in sickness and in health. Walking home, couldn't help thinking of all the times we ended up heading back home at the end of the night, always the two of us, remember Carol? There was something there, something real, but we never realised it until it was too late. And I want to say, Carol, I'll always regret that forever. I missed my chance with you, it'll never come again, never. You leaving was my *Toy Story*. (If you really know me, Carol, you will know what I mean.)

Love you (too late)

Tony

To: Tony
From: Carol
Subject: Re: Barcelona

What was *that*? Since you ask, I'm in the Mediterranean, somewhere between Sicily and Malta, feeling nice and chilled after an extra-long pilates session (the instructor is a mate). You, on the other hand, are beneath your duvet in hangover hell if there's any justice in the world. Read what you sent to me last night and cringe, you sad man. And what's all this *Toy Story* stuff about? Get a grip, Mr Potato Head.

Carol

To: Carol
From: Tony
Subject: Re: Barcelona

It seems I overdid it a bit last night. Sorry.

   Toy Story was the last film I rented out before I closed my video shop. I think I was trying to say that it was the end of an era. I've got a thumping headache and it's all a bit hazy to be honest (alcohol often brings on my migraine).

   OK, so the drink was talking, but I still mean it. Haven't been able to stop thinking about us since I got home. Do you think it's too late to work something out?

Tony

To: Tony
From: Carol
Subject: Re: Barcelona

So you've been thinking about Barcelona. Well, snap. Trouble is, the question that came to mind wasn't 'is it too late?' It was 'where does Lucy fit into all this?' Remember her? You should do, cos if she hadn't shaken you off at the airport, you'd be backpacking through Argentina with her right now. (Got an e-mail from Buenos Aires last week. Sends her love.) Oh and PS, if I remember correctly, you also told her you'd loved her since the age of seven.

I admit that seeing you in Spain gave me a massive feeling of nostalgia and the 'us thing' was a nice daydream for a day or two. But if I could swap our 'moment' for a plate of sausage, bacon, eggs and fried bread, I would, cos if I'm honest with myself, I was more homesick than lovesick. Sorry if this sounds harsh, but Lucy is my best mate. I can't believe you've forgotten her – even you can't be that shallow.

Don't go off in a huff though, cos I like our chats.
Carol
PS Oh, and Finn tells me you're taking more than a landlord-ly interest in a student called Laura. So all in all, I think we're best filed under 'when hell freezes over', don't you?

To: Carol
From: Tony
Subject: Re: Barcelona

I don't think you mean that. I'd understand if you thought it was just a crazy holiday thing, and that I got carried away with the beauty of the place and the sangria. Well, maybe I did, but I meant what I said and I don't need a get-out clause. I did love Lucy but, like you said, she shook me off. We had a great relationship, but it came to an end. The difference with us is we've never given ourselves a chance to find out if it could work. That's all I'm asking for.
Tony
PS The Laura thing is friendly concern, that's all. Trust Finn. What did he say exactly?

To: Tony
From: Carol
Subject: Re: Barcelona

Hmm. Being your long-distance second best. I think I can do better than that somehow. Nice thought, though.
Carol
PS That you'd been doing your stuff in the kitchen for her. Speaking as your ex-flatmate, it must be pretty full-on for you to break your 'Christmas lunch only' rule.

To: Carol
From: Tony
Subject: Re: Barcelona

Are you being deliberately thick or what? That isn't what I said! Long-distance, OK, we can't do anything about that. But you're not second-best to anyone. I bet you think I'll forget you just because you're not here. It isn't going to happen, Carol. My life's changed since Barcelona and I like it this way. I'm not asking you to save yourself for me (Is this pilates instructor male or female, incidentally?) But if you ever come back to Chester, just tell me you'll meet me for a drink and a chat.
Tony
PS I'm just trying to educate her. She's got no idea how to feed herself. I just feel I've got a gift and it's my duty to pass it on.

To: Tony
From: Carol
Subject: Re: Barcelona

OK.
Carol
PS Did you use those actual words? Because if so, I think I've worked out why you're still just friends.
PPS Male. But oddly enough I seem to be doing the 'save yourself' thing without even trying.

I break into Laura's account. Don't know why she and Tony have never got it together, it's a match made in control freak heaven.

To: Laura
From: Aidan
Subject: (No subject)

Tried to ring you again last night, but some girl Anna said you were out. I heard you telling her what to say. Do you think I'm stupid? I'm just trying to talk to you, Laura. Why are you acting like you're better than me now? Because you're in college do you think you can treat people like dirt? Or have you got a short memory? I think you owe me a phone call at least.
Aidan

To: Aidan
From: Laura
Subject: Re: (No subject)

Where did you get my e-mail address? I asked you not to contact me again. I haven't opened your letters. You think I don't realise that you're going through a difficult time? I'm sorry, but it's up to you to sort yourself out. That's what I've done and I'm not looking to anyone for help. I've made a new start here. Everything that's happened is in the past and it's meaningless to me now. I had to be tough with myself, so I don't see why you should be any different. Don't bother trying to get in touch again.
Laura

Better than I expected, but she still isn't giving much away. Back to Tony. I scroll down to the older e-mails and try another one at random. Aha. I *knew* he must have a dark side...

To: Tony
From: LoveSugar
Subject: Your order

Thank you for ordering from our Sweet Desires range. We have despatched your party fun-tool, extension nozzle and wipe-clean rubber sheeting. £24.99 inc. postage and packing has been debited from your credit card account. Please order again.
Thanks
LoveSugar

Ah. As in *sugarcraft*.

> To: Tony
> From: Finn
> Subject: Stepdad says soz
>
> Tony, we have to sort this out. Your mum's upset about the way
> we've been carrying on and neither of us wants that, do we? You'll
> be pleased to know I won't be spending any more nights in your
> mum and dad's marital home. Vic is coming to live on the barge.
> I'm sorry that you feel I've treated you 'like a child' since I started
> seeing your mum. We are, of course, both mature adults and I hope
> we can discuss things in that spirit.
> Finn
> PS Found your Transformers in the airing cupboard, do you want to
> come and get them?

> To: Finn
> From: Tony
> Subject: Re: Stepdad says soz
>
> I've *so* had enough of your wisecracks. This whole relationship is a
> big guffaw to you, isn't it? Just remember I'm trying to save my
> mum from something that'll end in tears. If this amuses you, then
> so be it.
> Tony

> To: Tony
> From: Finn
> Subject: Re: Stepdad says soz
>
> Tony, chill out. I've got an idea. Why don't we spend some time
> together, just the two of us, and try and work out our differences
> like rational grown-ups? How about the zoo with ice cream
> afterwards?
> Finn

I can almost see Finn chuckling to himself as he wrote this. But then
he did pick the world's most easy-to-wind-up man. I skip the rest of
Finn's mail and find a name I don't recognise.

To: Mr Jackson, Renewable Waste Systems
From: Tony
Subject: Progress report

Dear Mr Jackson
Pleased to report that all is going smoothly with the water system.
Pressure levels are moderate and flow volume is holding steady. I
look forward to your inspection.

When contacting me by phone, please make sure you speak to
me in person. I am currently educating members of my household
about the system and I don't want them to be confused by
conflicting information.
Tony Hutchinson

That's 'educating' as in 'not telling them that they're drinking each
other's waste products'. I wish I'd found this a couple of weeks ago,
before everyone worked out what was happening. If I could have
exposed what he was up to, I'd have been a hero.

(Still, if I find out enough about Lewis, maybe I still could be.)
For now, I keep searching through Tony's dirty washing.

To: Aidan
From: Tony
Subject: Laura

Hello
Sorry to contact you out of the blue. You don't know me. I'm Laura
Burns's landlord in Chester. I saw your e-address on a letter that
had been left around the house. Laura doesn't know I have it and I
would be grateful if you didn't mention my contacting you. I only did
it because I felt there was no other route. I'm very worried about
Laura's eating habits. Most days, she seems to get by on porridge
and I'm sure you're aware this is far from a balanced diet. I've tried
to discuss it with her but she's a very private person. I need to know
whether she's ever suffered from an eating disorder, because if so,
I want her to get help. I know I've intruded on her privacy by writing
this, but I'd rather that than see her put her health at risk.
Tony Hutchinson

Nice. There's a risk involved in this – neither Tony nor Laura are the forgive-and-forget type, so if I'm caught, I'm over – but I don't care, this baby's going straight to Laura. Sweet dreams, Tone...

16 May 2001   2:05am

Not feeling so confident now. All day I've been worrying about the fallout from the e-mail I sent to Laura. I saw Tony at lunchtime and I'm sure he blanked me in an 'I'll deal with you later' kind of way.

> To: Tony
> From: Laura
> Subject: (No subject)
>
> I'm in college, supposed to be writing my essay, but this is eating away at me and I can't concentrate. I hope everything I said is still ringing in your ears. Still can't believe even you could stoop so low as to go through my letters. That would have been bad enough, but to e-mail someone as well? Who do you think you are? In case you've forgotten, all you are to me is someone I pay for a roof over my head. You know nothing about my life and you have no right to judge anything I do. Or am I still 'over-reacting'? I'll find out, won't I, once I've told everyone what you've done.
> Laura

> To: Tony
> From: Aidan
> Subject: Re: Laura
>
> Dear Tony
> Thank you for getting in touch. I am very concerned to hear that my friend Laura is not eating properly. She has had various problems in the past but I thought she was over them. I think it's best that I call to see her as soon as possible.
>   In the meantime, perhaps you can give me her new mobile number, as I have mislaid it. (You are right, Laura wouldn't want to

know that we are going behind her back, so it's best not to tell her
why you need it.)
Aidan

To: Aidan
From: Tony
Subject: Re: Laura

Aidan
It was a misunderstanding and it's all sorted. I really don't think you
being here would help Laura.
Tony

To: Laura
From: Tony
Subject: So sorry

Laura, I really am so sorry for the insensitive way I behaved. The
distress I have caused you will be reflected in a reduced rent bill for
the next two months. The last thing I want is a bad atmosphere in
the house. But there's no need to involve other people in this. I take
it you haven't told anyone yet?
Tony

I try to get into Laura's e-mails, but she's changed her password. At
least she's unlikely to make trouble if she wants to stay low profile.
Tony could be more of a problem. It was worth it just to see him
weasel his way out of trouble, but I feel like I've already used up a
couple of my lives on this, so I log off. I go through Lewis's e-mails,
but there's nothing new. I want to know whether Finn's picked up
any clues about what he's up to.

To: Carol
From: Finn
Subject: Hello

Hello Missus
Marmite on toast, smoky bacon crisps, proper telly, smell of fresh-
cut grass. Hopefully that's cancelled out all the things you were

going to mention to make *me* throw up with jealousy. So how's life? It's 3:30am and I should be cashing up (you're my tea-break before I do those pesky 1ps and 2ps). You asked me what I've been up to. Well, apart from working my butt off in this place, the flat's almost decorated. Hard work painting the ceilings, I got a stiff neck watching Victoria do it. (Don't worry, I bought her some stilts.) My beloved business partner is back, full of big ideas for this place. (Don't know whether I figure in any of them, but that's another story.)

Say hi to Indonesia for me.

Finn

PS I seem to remember you said I didn't sound too chirpy in my last e-mail. Is this any better?

To: Finn
From: Carol
Subject: Re: Hello

Hello Mister

I've just come off stage (been singing at this couple's fiftieth wedding anniversary party – soooo sweet but scary at the same time). Sorry, Marmite on toast? You must have got me mixed up with some other ex-girlfriend. Your list set me thinking, though. Remember one night we were in town having fish and chips and I said 'Let's go for a drive?' Well anyway, you said OK, but we got lost and ended up on that beach in north Wales at about two in the morning. (If you remember what happened next you shouldn't, you're a married man. Don't you dare read anything into this!) I suppose what I mean is, being on this ship, I'm getting to see the world, but I know where I'm going to be every day for the next three months. I miss just going somewhere, not knowing where I'm going to end up. Does this make any sense? I'll shut up now.

Carol

To: Carol
From: Finn
Subject: Re: Hello

Tell me about it. Do you realise you've just described being married?

Don't read anything into this, either.

Finn

PS You didn't answer my question.

To: Finn
From: Carol
Subject: Re: Hello

Whoops.

Carol

PS You sound like someone settled in a two-bedroom flat with his wife should sound. Don't know whether this is good or bad.

To: Ruth
From: Finn
Subject: Lewis

Lewis offered to buy me and Vicky out this morning. Has he said anything to you about this? I thought it was worth thinking about, but Vicky's totally gone off on one. They just had a major barney, which ended with Vic telling him he just wanted what he couldn't have. I feel kind of weird about it. Lewis is a good mate and everything, but we can't pretend things have been working lately. I've never thought about this before but now it's been said, it kind of makes sense. Me and Vic could go off somewhere else and start again with a new business. The thing is, Vic now sees it as a personal battle with Lewis. Need some of your cool, calm common sense ASAP please.

Finn

To: Finn
From: Ruth
Subject: Re: Lewis

You haven't mentioned the most obvious thing. Where would he get the money from?

Ruth

To: Ruth
From: Finn
Subject: Re: Lewis

True. I was so stunned by the whole buy-out thing I didn't think to
ask. I will, though.
Finn

It sounds to me like Ruth is starting to get suspicious of Lewis, at
least more so than Finn. I try again to break into her account but I
only succeed in wasting an hour. By then, I'm too wound up to go to
bed. I go into Geri's e-mails just for the entertainment value.

To: Anna
From: Geri
Subject: Posh girl on a power trip

I just wanted to thank you for listening to me rant on at lunchtime
and for nodding in the right places. Am I being totally unreasonable
or is Izzy the most infuriating woman on the planet? OK, so she
came up with the idea of games to raise funds for the magazine,
but since when was world domination part of the deal? I didn't even
want the hassle of organising a bunch of students running round
wearing over-sized heads (guess who won't need a costume) but
somehow I heard myself say I wanted to be captain of a team. So
now I'm doing something I don't want to, just to prove a stupid
point. What is it about her that brings out the worst in me? Don't
say Adam because that's so over. Did you see him agreeing with
her before she'd even finished talking? Funny how he always
played hard-to-get with me, but can't manage it with her.
    Do you know Dan Hunter? I think he does mechanical
engineering. I've spoken to him a few times but can't work out
what kind of vibe I'm getting from him. (At a push I'd say cool-
borderline-uninterested.) Maybe I'm losing my touch.
Geri
PS I took your advice and bought your dream book last week (like
getting out of bed wasn't hard enough already). It was spiders last
night. Apparently they're good luck, but tarantulas are supposed to

mean health problems. I got myself into a bit of a state worrying which ones I'd dreamt about. Almost went to the library to consult the *Bumper Book of Creepy Crawlies*, but managed to stop myself just in time to retain some self-respect.

To: Geri
From: Anna
Subject: Re: Posh girl on a power trip

At least you weren't around when Izzy talked us through her top ten leadership moments in the Brownies and Guides. Don't really know Dan Hunter but why bother if he doesn't seem interested? Either he really isn't or he's playing games with you. I know you like a challenge, but it sounds like you're asking to get hurt.
Anna
PS The book's been in my drawer since I realised all my dreams were about exam anxiety. *Four weeks* till my first one.

To: Anna
From: Geri
Subject: Re: Posh girl on a power trip

Maybe that's true, but I could say the same about you and Alex. I just hope he really has changed this time.
Geri

To: Chloe
From: Geri
Subject: Games

What was Izzy *like* today? OK, we've all seen your enthusiasm – can you put it away now please? Plus her head was so far up her own behind, I expected her belly button to start talking. I'm not asking you to sign your life away right now, but if you don't fancy the idea of getting bossed around by plummy-chops for the next few weeks, I'd really like to have you on my team. How's Matt? Haven't seen the two of you together for a few days. Is everything OK?
Geri

To: Geri
From: Chloe
Subject: Re: Games

OK, I'm with you, if only to avoid the embarrassment of waiting around to be picked (uh-oh, school netball-team flashback). We've got to come up with as many daft ideas as we can, otherwise Izzy's going to turn it into a mini-Olympics, only more competitive – I've already heard whispers about fitness training (shudder). As for Matt, we're still plodding along. We haven't had a home run yet, but he's an old-fashioned kind of boy and I think he wants to 'woo' me properly first. Still, it's a major novelty after Max and O.B.'s I've-bought-you-a-drink-now-let's-have-you approach, so I'm not complaining. I've been having some weird feelings lately, though (not sure if I should say this really). I've always got on really well with Theo, but this last week it's started to tip over into something else. Yesterday I put on a virtual reality headset that he'd just been trying out. It smelt of him and I came over 'all unnecessary' (as my mum would say). I suppose that's the danger of being cooped up in a high-tech novelty shop with a dangerously good-looking man. The trouble is, I don't leave him behind when I leave work. It's just I've never met anyone who's completely chilled about everything and seems to have his life all worked out. (I just know I'm going to come over all girly-crush next time I go in there now.) You're the expert – how do I get him out of my head?
Chloe

Just for a second I think about sending this to Matt. No, too cruel. Too dangerous, more like – if anyone's prepared to put in the time and effort to track me down, it's him. The college radio scam proved he's got the brains and the cunning. I find Theo's address by trawling Finn's e-mails and I send it to him instead.

17 May 2001   2:10am

Had a scary moment with Mandy today. She was heading back around 3:00am last night, after a night out with Ben, and she saw my desk light as she was walking past. She noticed the bags under my eyes and said I must be working too hard. I just agreed, cool as anything, but she's got me worried. Seems like a good reason to visit her first.

To: Mandy
From: Ben
Subject: Your business

I'm sorry about earlier. I was angry with Luke, not you. I just find it really hard to talk about this because it always ends up in a row. So I had a think and I started to write stuff down. This is what I was trying to say:
1. Luke knows how grateful to him you are for investing in your business and he's taking advantage of it by trying to muscle in.
2. I feel like you're being bullied but you're afraid to fight back.
3. You say this is because you don't want him to pull the money out. I think it's because you still feel guilty about us going behind his back.
4. Every time I try to say this, you deny it and say he's totally over you. (This is usually where the row starts.)
5. He so isn't. I know you won't accept this, but who spent hours with him listening to him talk about you while we were getting together? (Being with Laura doesn't mean he's moved on.)
6. I know that you're in college stressing about all this right now and I hate the way he keeps doing this to you.
7. I also hate what this is doing to us.
Ben

To: Ben
From: Mandy
Subject: Re: Your business

I'm sorry if I snapped at you. I just can't handle the way everything gets so complicated. Thanks for sending me your thoughts. Anyway, here are mine:
1. I am grateful to Luke. He wants to get involved because he needs to make money and the sooner the site's up and running, the sooner we'll get a return.

2. I don't do being bullied. (You should know me better than to say that.)

3. He could pull the money out if he wanted to. I won't let that happen because this site is important to me. If that means having to agree to some of his demands, fine.

4/5. I think he is over me and it's an insult to Laura to say she doesn't matter to him. But whatever his feelings are, they're his problem, not mine.

6. You're right, I am stressing, but it's because I'm trying to take on too much. If having Luke working with me takes some of the pressure off me, then I'll agree to it.

7. So do I. Of course I'd rather not work with Luke, but this is how things are and we're stuck with them. Please try to understand.
Mandy

To: Mandy
From: Ben
Subject: Re: Your business

OK, I hear you Mand. I think it's time we made up, don't you? Dad's going up to Newcastle tonight and won't be back till tomorrow, so we won't have to squeeze into my kiddie bed (and I won't have to sleep on the floor). I've got some wine and I'll ring for pizzas, you can bring the sexy stuff and the chocolate sauce. Deal?
Ben

To: Ben
From: Mandy
Subject: Re: Your business

Deal.
Mand
PS Chocolate sauce? That's a bit last month, isn't it? I thought we were onto squirty cream now?

That's going *straight* to Abby. I read on.

To: Cindy
From: Mandy
Subject: Hi

How are you? Hugs and kisses to Holly for her brilliant drawing of us lot back in Chester (Gordon was chuffed that she drew him with hair). Luke's being a real pain again, just when I thought it was all over with. He wants to work with me on the website. He says it's so the work can get done quicker, but I'm really not sure about him. Haven't given him an answer yet, but he knows he's got me in a trap because of the money he's put in. The worst thing is I have to keep telling Ben that Luke is over me when I'm not convinced myself. We've been having loads of arguments. The frustrating thing is that I think Ben's probably right. Most of the time I'm angry with Luke, but Ben's the one I take it out on. (Still, at least we get to do plenty of making up!)

Lewis sends his love. He says he wants to buy Finn out of the club. He thinks Finn is holding him back and that he really wants to 'be someone'. It's weird, he seems to be doing really well but nothing he's got seems to be good enough for him. I think Mum's a bit worried about him. I don't know whether he'd be able to cope with the club without Finn.

Hope Jude is OK (has she sorted out her love life yet?)
Love
Mandy
PS Did Ben ever bring his uniform home when you were going out with him? Just want to know if it's allowed, but don't want to ask and sound stupid!

To: Mandy
From: Cindy
Subject: Re: Hi

So Lewis isn't at all like his sister then?! You're hardly into settling for less yourself, are you? Otherwise you'd tell Luke where to stick his money and you wouldn't be having all these traumas. Is it really worth it?

As for Jude, don't even go there. She's just had a massive row with Benicio (she threw a shoe at him and smashed a mirror. I

found Holly trying to play with the bits of glass – Jude doesn't do sweeping up). I think he's found out about her and Javier. Jude's locked herself in her bedroom, I've tried ringing her on her mobile but she won't talk to me. Don't tell Dad. I'm really angry with her because Holly was terrified and she could've cut herself really badly. We've spent most of the day down at Pete's bar just to get some peace. (Don't worry, I'm not dragging Holly to a pub, it's right on the beach.)
Cindy
PS And this question has nothing to do with 'making up', I suppose?!
(No, I don't think he's supposed to, but yes he did, twice (!))

Uh-oh. Just did something really stupid. I leaned back too far in my chair and over-balanced. I threw my arm out to the side and managed to grab the radiator, but the chair still crashed to the floor. I'd better log off in case anyone comes knocking. I sit for a few minutes with 'work' on the screen, just to be on the safe side. No one comes, so I log back on and enter Lisa's e-mails. I've been meaning to catch up with her for days.

To: Lisa
From: Zara
Subject: London

Has your dad signed the consent form for the London trip yet? Don't forget!!! It's going to be wicked, Jade Bryant in Year 11 went last year and she reckons the museums only take about three hours, then we can go and punish the shops (Steph knows where they've got the whole Urban Decay range ☺ and they don't hassle you when you try stuff out). Just don't let your dad say no, tell him there's coursework based on it which is compulsory. I'm not putting pressure on you but only the really square people won't go. Plus if you don't, you'll have to put up with Abby going on about it forever.
Za

To: Kim
From: Lisa
Subject: Miracle

Have to tell you about this because it's so unbelievable… I asked Dad if I could go on a school trip to London – museums and stuff, and we're staying overnight – and he said yes. Zara, etc. are all going and I know this sounds immature, but I'm really excited! I asked him twice, just in case it was temporary insanity, but he was definitely OK with it. Got to go, someone needs the computer. See you!

Lisa

PS Something weird happened, there was this e-mail I hadn't read but it had been opened. Do you think it might have been Dad checking up on me?

To: Kim
From: Lisa
Subject: (No subject)

It's 9:15pm and I've been in my room since I got home from school. Guess what. When I said it was unbelievable, I was right. Dad just blatantly lied to me. I asked him for the £40 to go to London and he said I couldn't have it because he has to buy a new whatever for the rally car (like he can't afford both). He couldn't even get his excuse straight, cos then he said he didn't want me staying away overnight. So I'm officially the afterthought in this family. The one who doesn't count. The one anyone can lie to just to shut me up. Dan was there but (big surprise) he didn't back me up – it's just like having another Dad. Neither of them gave a toss how I felt. I hate my dad for what he's doing to me. I bet it was him who read my e-mail. And now I hate myself for blaming him. Why does my life have to be so screwed up? I can't live like this any more. God knows what I'm going to tell them at school. I feel like I'm being punished for something that wasn't my fault and I've had it up to my neck. Sorry to dump all this crap on you, Kim.

Lisa

I feel like going round to Lisa's house and asking her dad what his problem is. There's something really strange about that family, something not right that really bothers me. Most of all, I want to know what Lisa feels she's being punished for. But I just heard someone walking around on the landing. As I'm debating whether to log off, a thought comes to me – what happened with that e-mail I helpfully re-routed to Theo?

To: Geri
From: Chloe
Subject: Bizarre shameful crush

Such a weird shift at Theologic today. Theo had loads of new orders to unpack, so thankfully I didn't have time to burst into girlish giggles at his every word and/or follow him around like a lost kitten, which I would otherwise have done. Maybe this is just my sixth crush-sense, but he seemed really odd with me. He kept coming out with these Zen-like phrases about the wise man overcoming desire and how we pursue that which flees from us. It freaked me out a bit, to be honest.

Anyway, I got home to find Matt waiting for me. He said he had a surprise and he gave me the DVD of *Sleepy Hollow*, which is the coolest present ever for the following reasons: (a) I've wanted it for ages, (b) Matt hates Johnny Depp but knows I love him, and (c) it wasn't even my birthday or anything. (Haven't got a DVD player, but we can go round to Mum and Dad's.) He gave me a bit of a cuddle and said he bought it because he thought I'd been a bit stressed out about the exams. He is the sweetest, best man I have ever known and how guilty do I feel? Please note that I will never, ever have a bizarre crush again (unless of course it's the Deppster himself on horseback and gagging for a lusty, red-haired wench).
Chloe

Who knows, I might have saved Matt and Chloe's relationship. I don't want anything to spoil the mood this puts me in, so I log off. For the first time in months I can go to bed feeling good about myself.

28 May 2001   1:15am

A lot to catch up on. Real life has kept me away from the computer for too long. I dive into Lewis's e-mails and come up with this, dated three days ago:

> To: Gerry
> From: Kurt
> Subject: My contact no.
>
> I understand there was some confusion when you tried to contact me on my home number. Can you please tell me what your inquiry was about? This address is at my office and it's the best way to get hold of me if you need to contact me again.
> Kurt Benson

There's no reply. Who's Gerry? I stare at the message for a few minutes. When I blink I can still see the shape of the lines under my eyelids, glowing purple. I should confront him. I'm the only one who knows anything about what he's doing, and that makes it my duty to act.

But what is he doing, exactly? He's using Kurt's name, but why? I feel so sorry for Ruth. Say I did the brave thing and confronted him – I know that he'll be able to talk his way out of it. If he's got this far, he's bound to have a cover story. If I challenge him, all I'll be doing is driving him further underground. I have to keep watching and waiting until he's revealed a bit more of himself. There's another e-mail, sent today.

> To: Finn
> From: Lewis
> Subject: Victoria
>
> Just in case you get this before I see you next, tell Victoria not to bother mentioning it again. Nice attempt to turn the tables by offering to buy me out, but sorry, it's not going anywhere and neither am I. I know this is totally Victoria's idea and the last thing

you want is more responsibility. Think of what your life could be like
if I bought you out. You'd have money and the freedom to do what
you wanted. I know you can talk her round, you just haven't tried
hard enough.
Lewis

This sounds desperate, even for Lewis. I go to Geri's e-mails to see
if I can find out more about the phone call for Kurt.

To: Geri
From: Anna
Subject: I think I'm dying

Haven't seen you around yet, so I assume you're still at Ruth's. I'm
in the media lab, not sure whether I'm hungover or still drunk. (The
lights are so bright in here.) It's the only place I can find which is
warm. Can't believe all my stuff's been ruined and I'm living on a
barge, all because Tony's an idiot. Apparently it could be weeks
before we're allowed back into the house. Anyway, you're probably
wondering why I'm telling you all this. I just felt I had to share last
night's experience with you. Ended up at a dinner party at Finn and
Victoria's flat. What a nightmare. It was all the older people on one
side talking about double glazing and the best route to Cornwall,
the rest of us on the other side drinking as fast as we could to stop
the nervous giggles. I think I insulted at least two people really
badly, but can't remember who or how (I think it was something
subtle along the lines of ha ha, you're old, I'm not). Felt really sorry
for Finn. Just hope every mealtime isn't like that for them. Oh the
canteen's just opened. Need bacon.
Anna

To: Anna
From: Geri
Subject: Re: I think I'm dying

From the sound of you I'm thinking drunk more than hungover, not
that I'm judging... Anyway, it was a nice surprise to hear from you.
Sorry you're in a state. I've also had a bit of a weird time today. I had
the recurring nightmare I told you about, where I'm climbing

higher and higher up a flight of stairs and then I fall. Only this time, it felt like I was watching from the top floor and I could kind of see myself lying dead in the stairwell. I was looking it up in the book and the phone rang. Ruth had already left, so I got it. This is the weird part. It was a bloke asking for Kurt Benson. That's Ruth's former husband, and he died two years ago almost to the day. Ruth was telling me how much she misses him the other night. It could have been a sick joke, but the caller sounded really serious. I didn't tell him Kurt was dead. I haven't told Ruth about the call either. I don't know how. I mentioned it to Lewis and he said it must just have been some mistake. But it didn't feel that way.

Anna, if Ruth's out this evening, do you mind calling round? The thought of being in the flat on my own really spooks me out. (By the way, it's all your fault. I'm starting to wish I'd never come across that book.)
Geri

None of this surprises me after Lewis's e-mail, but it's still a shock to read it. My conscience isn't so much pricking me as stabbing me with a steak knife. My heart goes out to Ruth and I'm so relieved Geri knows how devastated she would be if she knew. I really, *really* have to do something. I try Finn's e-mail to see if he's cottoned on to anything.

To: Ruth
From: Finn
Subject: Lewis

Help. My head's going to explode. I'm caught in a warzone between my beloved wife and my beloved business partner. How come the two most stubborn people in the world ended up getting involved with a Mr Easy-Going like me? Maybe I should just walk out and leave them to it, because if ever there were two of a kind, it's them. Don't know what to do. Dread going in to work these days. If I say Lewis has a point, Vic bites my head off, and if I stand up for Vic, blah blah blah. This so wasn't why I wanted to own a club. Might be able to escape for an hour or two this afternoon. If so, fancy a beer?
Finn

No reply from Ruth; she probably phoned him. All I find is this:

To: Finn
From: Tony
Subject: Buyout

Mum's told me about her plan to buy out Lewis. So how's it going? I
think she's doing the right thing. It'll be a bit tricky for you, what
with Lewis being your mate, but Mum's got good ideas for that
place and you know what they say about too many cooks. Make
sure you get a good solicitor to look at the contracts.
Tony

To: Tony
From: Finn
Subject: Re: Buyout

Knowledge and information, mate – they're two different beasts. If
you'd really spoken to your mum, instead of overhearing her on the
phone, you'd know that it all depends on Lewis. As you're so keen
to stick your nose where it doesn't belong, heard any more from
Louise since your non-date at the beach? Carol sends her love by
the way.
Finn

I pass this on to Carol, just because I want to know whether she'll be
jealous. Although I've read all her e-mails to Tony, I can't work out
whether she feels anything for him or just enjoys flirting. I don't
think Tony knows either, so maybe this will do him a favour. Yeah,
right. I should log off now. Maybe just one more...

To: Kim
From: Lisa
Subject: Panic

I signed the consent form for London and handed it in. I didn't
mean to, but Zara borrowed the £40 for me and I couldn't say no.
Just my nightmare luck, Dan came into school to bring my PE kit
which I'd 'accidentally' forgotten (cheers Dan, for a minute I
thought I wouldn't be able to spend 70 minutes sweating while

scary, hairy Mary screams at me not to run away from the ball.
(See what I mean about him being my second Dad?)) Anyway, he
saw that I'd forged Dad's signature and warned me not to hand it
in, which of course I then did. Part of me wants to get on the coach
and teach Dad a lesson, but I know I'd be hurting him and I don't
want to, I just want to do something normal for once. I can't not go,
Kim. Everyone's talking about it 24/7, especially Zara and Abby,
and I know things are going to be a million times worse than they
are already if I'm too 'square' to go. Oh, and by the way, 'we' leave
tomorrow. What am I going to do?
Lisa

If I could fast-forward the next twenty-four hours, I'd be there. It's
not that I'm addicted, it's just that the rest of my life seems more and
more drab and uninteresting compared to the couple of hours I
spend at this screen. It's like stepping out from an old, black and
white film, slap bang into *The Matrix*. I log off and go over to the
window. I stare out for a while not thinking of anything, then I catch
my reflection. It feels like my conscience staring back at me, waiting
to see if I'll do the right thing. I go to bed.

29 May 2001   2:35am

To: Ruth
From: Finn
Subject: Phone call

If you're still up (and I bet you are), go to bed, it's 2:10am. (Why do I
always get the urge for a chat when I'm cashing up the coppers?)
You're probably thinking about the phone call for Kurt and asking
yourself loads of questions you can't answer. You're telling yourself
you think about things too much, but it isn't helping. So I'm going to
do it for you, OK? Ruth, there are thousands of people who must
have had his name. You know how companies pass details on. Not
all of them will know what's happened. Knowing you're all wound

up is making me all wound up. Please try to chill. Or I'm going to need a cocoa or something.
Finn

To: Finn
From: Ruth
Subject: Re: Phone call

Yes, you guessed it. I was doing preparation for a lecture (honest). I've sort of told myself all the things you just said, but it helped to hear them from someone else. It's the way whoever was calling wouldn't accept it when I said Kurt was dead that really upset me (but I suppose people who make calls for a living get fed up with crap excuses – 'he's dead' – 'yeah right'). I am wound up, but not just about the call. It was the way Lewis reacted when I came to talk to you earlier, like I should have gone to him. He acted like he had the right to be offended. At first I was touched that he was concerned about me, but I've realised it was just a typical Lewis ego game. Anyway, I'll stop now. I hate talking about him behind his back.
Ruth

To: Ruth
From: Finn
Subject: Re: Phone call

Don't know what to think about Lewis any more. It's not great having to work with someone who wants to get rid of you. Haven't asked him where he'd get the money to buy us out, cos he'd think I was interested. The thing is, I've got worries about him, but I don't know whether they're my worries or Victoria's. Is this what marriage has done to me?

I know what you mean about speaking your mind. I've got into this habit of editing everything before I say it (keeps me out of a lot of trouble). Sometimes, though, I wish I could just be honest. You've probably heard about the dinner party we had the other night. Vicky got a bit mardy when I brought loads of people round. I got all defensive, but I should've just been honest and told her I wanted to be with people my own age. But I felt like I couldn't, in case she

Dad, I made a mistake but don't ever think it's like father, like son. I'll never let myself become what you are.

Who'd send me flowers in Kurt's name? I'm coming up with new suspects all the time.

Seems Izzy isn't content with taking Adam, she wants to take my memories as well – Geri.

Our music reflects the daily struggle to survive in the harsh urban environment where we were born and raised.

I thought you understood
how much Holly means to
me, but I was so wrong.
Thanks for nothing – Cindy.

We've never given ourselves a
chance to find out if it could work.
That's all I'm asking for – Tony.

Abby may be my friend but she's also a two-faced cow. I'm not giving her the satisfaction of thinking I'm bothered – Zara.

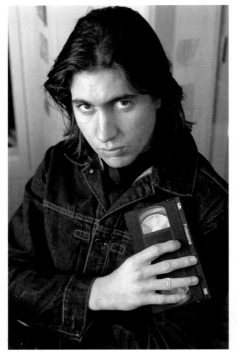

I've made a huge balls-up Iz, and I'm really sorry. Geri got involved by accident and I wish she hadn't.

You know nothing about my life and you have no right to judge anything I do.

The worst thing is, I have to keep telling Ben that Luke is over me when I'm not convinced myself – Mandy.

At lunch, I was single and together. Now I'm half a couple and all over the place. Work that one out – Anna.

If I don't deliver that girl the biggest ass-whupping of her pampered existence then shoot me – Geri.

How come the two most stubborn
people in the world ended up with
a Mr Easy-Going like me – Finn.

Ruth, I just want you to know
it's the first thought on my mind
when I wake up, and it probably
always will be – Lewis.

I hate my dad for what he's doing to me. And now I hate myself for blaming him. Why does my life have to be so screwed up? – Lisa.

Totally selfish I know, but what I really want to do is get away from Luke and Ben and let them sort it out.

took it the wrong way. How stupid is that? Anyway, she won't thank me for chatting to you when I should be warming up the marital bed.
Laters
Finn

I try Tony's account to find out what Carol's made of his 'date'.

To: Tony, Finn
From: Carol
Subject: Gosh

Gosh, look what I've received accidentally on purpose. Tony's got a date! Well done, Finn, for pointing that out to me. Tony, you really outwitted me there, you sly so-and-so! Telling me you love me, then going after someone else when I'm only two thousand miles away!! I could've walked in and caught you at it, you daredevil!! And this is in addition to Miss This-is-how-you-boil-an-egg, well done!! I'll leave you both to pat yourselves on the back (and maybe do a little growing up).
Carol

To: Carol
From: Tony
Subject: Re: Gosh

Carol, this is Finn twisting the truth as usual. There was no 'date'.

To: Tony
From: Carol
Subject: Re: Gosh

What do you mean, there was no 'date'?

To: Carol
From: Tony
Subject: Re: Gosh

There was no date! She didn't turn up! And it was only supposed to be a friendly thing anyway. You have to believe me on this one, Carol.

To: Tony
From: Carol
Subject: Re: Gosh

So there would have been a date, only she stood you up. Thank you Tony, my self-esteem has now been restored to its usual level.

To: Carol
From: Tony
Subject: Re: Gosh

Carol, you've got this all wrong. Louise was just a friend I was going to spend the day with. It never crossed my mind that she could be anything more. I meant every word I said in Spain. I've never connected with any girl like I have with you, spiritually or physically. There's a big hole in my life and it'll always be there until you come back to Chester.
Yours as always
Tony

To: Tony
From: Carol
Subject: Re: Gosh

There's a big hole in your head and it doesn't half come out with some sentimental crap. (Physically? Excuse me, Barcelona only partly makes up for Newquay.) Tony, I don't care if you see someone else. I think it was you who said you didn't expect me to 'save myself' (because of course, this *is* the 1890s). (For the record, I have.) I *do* care if you creep around thinking you have to keep things from me. I thought the whole idea of keeping in touch was that we'd have some common ground when (or maybe if) I come home. That's not going to happen if you don't tell me what's going on in your life, is it? I know Finn can be a tinker, but there's one way round it – why don't you confide in me instead of him for a change?
Carol

To: Finn
From: Tony
Subject: Red-handed

Bet you thought you were hilarious telling Carol about my date,
didn't you? Mr Mischief-maker, making amusing mischief for his
friends, oh yeah, someone please sew up my sides! Well, if
anything, it's brought us closer together – not quite what you
intended, is it?
Tony

To: Tony
From: Finn
Subject: Re: Red-handed

What the hell are you on about, you freak of nature? Don't you think
I've got better things to do than mess around with your Fantasy
Girlfriend League?

I chew the last few bits of my microwave popcorn and read through
these e-mails again. Unless Finn's a smarter cookie than I've given
him credit for, there's no danger of him smelling a rat. I head for
Lisa's e-mail account. I've been saving this up.

To: Zara
From: Lisa
Subject: (No subject)

If you're reading this, it must be Tuesday and you're home. Hope
you had a good time in London. I bet you're still talking about
what happened tonight on the bus. So would I, if some other girl's
dad did what mine did. But it was my fault for forging his
signature on the form. I just really wanted to go but I should have
listened to him, should have known something like that would
happen. Now it's all backfired on me and I just hope no one
thinks you and Abby are as weird as I am because you were
sitting with me. Sorry.
Lisa

To: Lisa
From: Zara
Subject: Re: (No subject)

It's not Tuesday, it's tonight (there's this lad, Steve, in the hostel who's letting us use his laptop. Abby has promised to make it 'worth his while'. Hmm). Why are you sorry? It wasn't your fault, Lisa. Are you OK? Your dad was really off it, I thought he was going to punch Miss Hawkins when she tried to stop him. I know he's your dad but he had no right to treat you like that. Hope you had a go at him when you got home. Got to go before Abby makes a complete tart of herself (whoops, too late). Sorry you couldn't come, I'll try and get you some Urban Decay. See you.
Zara

To: Kim
From: Lisa
Subject: Dad

I hate my dad. I've tried not to, but I can't help it. You won't believe what he did. I decided to go on the trip. I was on the bus with the others and we were about to leave when Dad comes on, shouting and yelling at me. Then he dragged me off in front of everyone, like they were trying to kidnap me. (Guess who was waiting in the car, Dad two, of course, accusing me of trying to give Dad a heart attack.) Zara was really shocked, but Abby just had this look on her face like I was from another planet. I've never felt so humiliated and crap in my life.

I thought maybe if I did something I want for once, I could go back to being the person I was. As if. Zara's OK about it, but the way I feel, I never want to see any of them again. (Bet they feel the same about me.)
Lisa

I go into Steph's e-mail to see if she's right.

To: Steph
From: Abby
Subject: Lisa

Has Zara e-mailed you yet? Hope not, cos I've got loads of juicy news, you won't believe what happened b4 – Lisa got pulled off the coach by her dad! He was like, you are *so* busted!! He chucked a massive loopy and threatened to call the police. Everyone was like, yeah, please do, cos you're a complete mentalist, mate. Her brother was waiting outside (slurp, his butt is so gr8, I swear it gets firmer every time he points it in my direction). She was so embarrassed I almost felt sorry for her.

The hostel's really cool, it's got all-girl dorms but mixed floors. Steve, the lad who lent us the laptop, is blond, good bod but his eyebrows meet in the middle – wish I'd brought my leg wax. We're waiting until Miss Hawkins has gone to bed, then Steve reckons he can get us into this club where some of Papa Roach were last week. Almost forgot... Party round at mine next weekend! Dad's away with work and Ben can't say anything cos I've found out he's been doing it with Mandy in Dad's bed. He only sent me one of his pervy e-mails by accident! (No you can't have a copy cos you'll change all the Mandys to Stephs, you dirty cow!!!)
Luv
Ab

To: Abby
From: Steph
Subject: Re: Lisa

No way! Did Lisa and her dad have a row, or did she just go? What did she say to him? You're so rubbish at e-mails!!
Steph

There's so much more I want to know about Lisa and her dad. Why is he so hard on her and why does her brother always take his side? So many questions, so little time: it's now 3:30 and my brain's starting to shut itself down.

It's now 3:50. I just woke up with my cheek on the desk. Yeuch, I've drooled all over my keyboard.

31 May 2001   2:11am

Big drama in Hollyoaks over the last twenty-four hours. A load of
bricks fell off the scaffolding outside Steam Team while Lewis and
Victoria were standing underneath. Lewis managed to push
Victoria to safety, but it was a close thing. The talk in Deva was
how Lewis saved Victoria's life by a split second. It feels strange,
watching the focus of my attention become the centre of everyone
else's thoughts as well.

> To: Lewis
> From: Tony
> Subject: Thank you
>
> Just heard what's happened. (I tried to phone you but there was no
> reply.) How can I ever find the words to thank you? Count yourself
> lucky I couldn't find you because I'd be hugging you right now.
> We've had our ups and downs, but I owe you everything. My future
> kids will look to you as the man who gave them their grandma.
> Come into Deva tomorrow and choose as many items as you like
> from the all-day breakfast menu. It's all yours, on me.
> Tony

> To: Lewis
> From: Finn
> Subject: What you did
>
> What I said to you tonight didn't come out right. There was loads
> more I wanted to say, but to be honest, mate, I was afraid of losing
> it. I can't say this stuff face-to-face unless I put on a funny voice or
> something, so Hallelujah for e-mail. Anyway, here goes. The fact is,
> you saved the person I love more than anyone else in the world. I
> don't even know how to start repaying you. I just hope this will help
> us forget all the bad times we've had. I've had a go at you about
> going off on your travels, but this has reminded me why you're my
> best mate. You've always put yourself on the spot for me. Thank
> you. Call the cliché police if you like, but I mean it from the bottom

of my heart. I'll always owe you. Sorry to ramble on but it helps me block out the thought of what might have happened if you hadn't been there.

Cheers mate. (Now I'll pass you over to someone else who wants a word...)

Hi Lewis. Well, what can I say? Thank you so much for being there. I feel so grateful for being able to write this. I'm going to try to get some rest now. Maybe you should do the same. I'm sure you had just as nasty a shock as I did.
Victoria

I get the old feeling, the hairs-standing-on-my-neck sensation I had when I first read Lewis's e-mails. Finn means every word, but Victoria seems distinctly cool for a woman who's just had her life saved. More grateful for being alive than grateful to Lewis. That last line, especially: 'I'm sure you had just as nasty a shock as I did.' It's almost as if she thinks he knew it was coming.

More than ever before, I'm desperate to pin Lewis down, to force him to tell me what he's really up to. I want to tell someone about my suspicions, in the hope that they'll share them and talk to other people, so that eventually the consequences of whatever Lewis has done will come crashing down on him. Pure wishful thinking. What would really happen is Lewis would become even more secretive than he is now. So I have to keep watching. And to do that, I have to stay invisible.

To: Finn, Tony
From: Lewis
Subject: (No subject)

Hope Victoria is feeling better. Finn – anyone would have done the same. Tone – thanks for the things you said, but I don't want to make a big thing of this, mate.
Lewis

I scroll back to the day before the brick incident and find this:

To: Ruth
From: Lewis
Subject: Finn

Hope you're OK. Ruth, it feels a bit weird asking you this, but I know Finn confides in you. Is there anything seriously wrong between Finn and Victoria? I've picked up odd vibes here and there. I tried to discuss it with him, but Victoria went off on one about interfering in their marriage. Now I can't mention it. One or two things have happened that make me think things aren't going too well. I just want to be put in the picture before it affects the business. Cheers.
Lewis

To: Lewis
From: Ruth
Subject: Re: Finn

Sounds like the business is already affected if you're afraid to talk to your partner. I don't really know what you're getting at and I don't feel comfortable getting involved.
Ruth

To: Ruth
From: Lewis
Subject: Re: Finn

I think what you mean is that you do know, but you don't want to tell me. Fine.
Lewis

I check Finn's e-mails to see if there's any mention of these 'one or two things'.

To: Finn
From: Ruth
Subject: Lewis

Got a strange e-mail from Lewis tonight, asking if I know anything about problems between you and Victoria. He said 'one or two things have happened' which made him wonder. No idea what he

means. It's not like him to nose about, so I thought I ought to tell you.
Ruth

To: Ruth
From: Finn
Subject: Re: Lewis

You know, just stuff. I've always reckoned a trouble shared is a trouble doubled. Don't want to go on about it cos it'll bore you and you won't want to talk to me ever.
Finn

A colleague of Ben Davies's was killed while the two of them were putting out a house fire. I check his e-mails but he's sent nothing since it happened. I try Mandy.

To: Cindy
From: Mandy
Subject: Hello

A lad Ben works with died in a fire today. They were in this house when the stairs collapsed and the lad, Chris, got trapped. Ben tried to get near enough to pull him out but the flames forced him back. Ben's staying here tonight, but he's with his dad at the moment. It was my idea, I thought he should speak to someone who knows what it's like to lose a colleague. He's so upset. He kept saying it was his fault because he's not experienced. I know this isn't true, but I don't know what to do except reassure him. I can't even do that properly, because what do I know about being in a fire? I feel bad because I'm sort of dreading him coming round now.

This is going to sound trivial now, but Laura's starting to get to me. Me and Ben had a row before all this happened, and she wouldn't stop going on about it, kept asking me why I wouldn't take his calls. I tried to tell her to stay out of it but she wouldn't take the hint. The worst thing is that I can't shut her up because it'll make things a nightmare with Luke and the website. I keep having all these (to put it politely) negative thoughts about her, then going on a guilt trip because it's just the way she is.

I think I just heard Mum letting Ben in. Hope you're all well.
Love
Mandy

To: Mandy
From: Cindy
Subject: Re: Hello

Mand, stop stressing. You're helping just by being with him. I bet he
doesn't want you to know what it was like, he wants you to listen.
Tell him I'm really sorry and I'll e-mail him soon.
Cind
PS Re Laura, that is so you, feeling guilty because someone else is
being a pain. Why don't you just tell her where to get off? She'll
probably respect you more.

All this depressing stuff is getting me down. I'm in desperate need
of some light relief.

To: Max
From: O.B.
Subject: You div

Just had Chloe asking me if 'it' was official and whether I'd just
been pretending when I went out with her! What have you been
saying? You've obviously stood there in the canteen going 'do you
want gravy, and by the way, did you know O.B. does it with blokes?'
What were you trying to do, Johnny No-Stars, reduce the
competition? Well bad luck, cos the kind of girls I'm going to be
with in Drama Society are the experimental type. They'll get a buzz
out of taking me to bed, just so they can tell their mates they turned
me straight.
O.B.

To: O.B.
From: Max
Subject: I want you now big boy

Hi, you naughty love-stud. You were brilliant at the auditions today.
The way you followed me round like a lost puppy, brown-nosed me

and agreed with everything I said drove me completely animal for your bod. Your performance was so intense and passionate, and I loved how you kept your eyes fastened to my jumper-melons, that takes real acting skill that does. You're definitely 'in' with me, laddie, I'm not laughing at you at all, honest, because you're so not desperate!
Izzy XXXX (And then you woke up.)

To: Max
From: O.B.
Subject: Re: I want you now big boy

At least I didn't lose my place when I was reading and make a total willy of myself.

    Izzy's well into me, mate. Oh yeah, look at me, I'm so desperate. 'Help, help, I'm drowning in a sea of bird. Send tea and sandwiches please, Mr Canteen Boy, we need to keep our strength up.'
O.B.

I think I'll send this to Izzy, then head for her mail.

To: Mandy
From: Izzy
Subject: Training

I was disappointed that you couldn't make training today. I just think it's a shame when people can't be bothered to turn up after the effort I've gone to.
Izzy

To: Izzy
From: Mandy
Subject: Re: Training

My boyfriend's colleague was killed in a fire; you may have read about it in the paper. I'm sure you understand that he's my priority at the moment. If you have a problem with this, maybe it's better that I pull out of your team altogether.
Mandy

To: Sis-sis
From: Izzy
Subject: Hi from your baby sis

It's *so* tedious to be surrounded by people who want you to fail. I feel like the whole college has resented me since I made the radical suggestion that we should get off our butts and do something to save the magazine instead of moaning about it. I had to cancel today's training session because everyone had a genuine-sounding (not) excuse. Plus all the costumes were wrecked in Tony's stupidity-induced pooh flood. The thing that really gets me is that everyone wants Adam to film the event. When I pointed out the glaringly obvious, they all turned on me. I mean, *hello*? Do these people have the memory spans of goldfish, or what? Of course, Geri was his biggest defender. She's set herself up as Mrs Nice to my Mrs Nasty, trying to make out I'm a power fiend who's forcing everyone past their limits. I came home today, locked myself in my room and had a good wah. I'm just trying to make the day a success. Why does everyone hate me for it? (Honest now, Sis-sis, am I really that bossy?)

   The drama soc. is the total opposite, really good fun. We've been auditioning for *The Changeling*. Remember I told you about those two lads who did that terrible rap record? Well they came and read for the male lead. One was pretty dire but the other really had something.
Love and hugs
Iz .

Which was which? This is so frustrating.

5 June 2001   1:20am

The *Chester Herald* had been full of Lewis, hailing him as the local hero who saved a life. There was a big photo of Lewis sitting with Victoria, both trying their best to smile. Underneath, there was a smaller picture of Finn and Tony patting Lewis on the back, while Lewis wears the same forced grin.

To: Lewis
From: Mandy
Subject: My hero

Just turned the radio on in the kitchen and guess who was talking?
You sounded so serious! They called you a 'local nightclub owner',
which made you sound about fifty (no one calls them *night*clubs
any more). Anyway, congratulations on your new celebrity, sign the
book/record/telly deals while you can!!
Love
Mand

To: Lewis
From: Cindy
Subject: Hero

Mandy told me what happened (Holly's doing a crayon version of it
right now. You've got blue hair. And you're wearing *verrrry* tight
trousers. Pink as well. Something you want to tell me?) Well, well –
never knew you had it in you! Seriously, well done, it was really
brave. God, what about Tony, is he trying to have your babies now?
Jude's just come in. She says she always knew you'd amount to
something eventually (!)
Love
Cindy and Holly (She'll send you her picture when it's finished.)

To: Gerry
From: Lewis
Subject: (No subject)

Really nice gesture, sending flowers to my mum. Leave her out of
this. It's my business and mine alone. What are you trying to
achieve?
Lewis

To: Dennis Richardson, c/o HMP Blackwood
From: Lewis
Subject: See attachment

Thought you might want to see this. No, that's a lie. I know you won't
want to see this, but I'm sending it to you anyway. Proof that I'm

nothing like you, Dad. Remember I said I was being tested before? Well, this was another test. To see whether I'm brave or a coward like you. Now everyone knows the answer because it's there in black and white. This makes up for what happened with Ruth. You never got the chance to make up for what you did but then you were never sorry, were you? Why don't you bribe someone to print this out for you, then put it up among the porno pictures in whatever filthy cage they've shoved you into. Then you can look at it every day and remind yourself of the person you'll never be.

Lewis

The attachment is a scanned-in copy of the *Chester Herald* article. I read these two e-mails again. Every part of my body feels restless, as if something's burrowed under my skin. It's one of those summer nights when nothing cools down. The heat in this room presses in on me and my skin's wet all over. If no one was around, I'd go for a walk down to the river, and I'd keep walking until all this made some kind of sense. I start to feel as though Lewis's secrets have imprisoned me.

There's more to it than that. Whatever Lewis's problem is, Ruth's been on the sharp end of it. What if I'm endangering her by staying silent? I feel like my head's full of fog. No matter how hard I try, I *can't* have a clear thought because there's too much to think about. *Lewis can't really be dangerous, can he?*

I can't hold off any longer. I send Lewis's e-mail to Ruth. I don't know what good it'll do. Maybe it'll make her realise that whatever she's been through, someone's looking out for her.

I'd better log off. Just a second, though – what happened to that O.B. e-mail I sent to Izzy?

To: O.B.
From: Izzy
Subject: Re: I want you now big boy

I assume this was some kind of pseudo-ironic, laddish attempt at a joke. Either that or you're taking method acting a step too far.

Izzy

To: Max
From: O.B.
Subject: You plum

What did you send that e-mail to Izzy for, you prat?

To: O.B.
From: Max
Subject: Re: You plum

What e-mail?

To: Max
From: O.B.
Subject: Re: You plum

What e-mail?! You know what e-mail, you tosser! The one about Izzy!

To: O.B.
From: Max
Subject: Re: You plum

So that'll be like *all* of them… What are you on about?

To: Max
From: O.B.
Subject: Re: You plum

Just learn how to use e-mail, you spanner.

6 June 2001   12:45am

I heard Ruth telling Lewis that she'd received flowers from 'Kurt Benson' this morning. I try and find out more from Finn. I'm dying to know what she's made of the Lewis e-mail I sent her.

To: Finn
From: Ruth
Subject: Thanks

Thanks for listening to me when I was in a state earlier. What makes me really angry is that I've wasted the whole day thinking about who might have done this. I'm coming up with new suspects all the time. This afternoon, I even thought they might be from Taylor (which is crazy). I feel more defensive towards Kurt than worried about myself. I have to keep reminding myself that someone is doing this to get at me, not Kurt's memory. Which isn't much comfort. Sorry to go on, Finn. It's just a relief to have someone I can talk to about it. Lewis made me feel like I was just wasting his time.

Another weird thing happened today. I got an e-mail from Lewis that was intended for his dad. (Remember you got one that time?) He was telling him about the falling bricks. Probably shouldn't say any more. It was just so angry it shook me up.

You and Vic have been on my mind this evening. I think it's what you were saying about having a baby. I didn't mean to be negative about it. I just got the feeling it was something you thought you should do, not something you want to do. But this has nothing to do with me, so...

Ruth

As I'm looking through Finn's sent mail, another item joins the list. Finn must be online. I log off for a few minutes, just in case I arouse suspicion, then go back in.

To:	Lewis
From:	Finn
Subject:	(No subject)

Tried to ring you, no answer. I'd be round your house now with my hands around your throat if I thought it'd do any good. I can't believe you told her about the other night. Why have you done this to me? You saved her life, now you want me to lose her – what's this about? You've been carrying this around, waiting for your moment, haven't you? Well do me a favour, mate, forget everything I said about you the other day. I wouldn't expect my worst enemy to do something as low as this.

Finn

What 'other night'? Has Finn slept with Ruth? It makes sense, after all – why else has she been taking such an interest in Finn and Victoria's baby plans? But if they had got it together and Lewis knew, I'd have heard about it by now, along with the rest of Chester. Still, it seems to fit with their closeness and the way they look to each other for support. I won't discount it until I've heard what really happened.

To: Lewis
From: Ruth
Subject: Your e-mail

Hi. You sent me an e-mail by accident last night. ('See attachment.') I assume it was meant for your dad. Surprised you think saving Victoria made up for what you did to me. So now you're a hero, all your unheroic behaviour is forgiven. Well, maybe in your mind. But I don't see why you think the two things are connected. What's done is done. OK, it's in the past, but don't ever think it'll be forgotten (or excused). The ironic thing is that I was totally over it until I saw this. You've probably guessed that I'm surprised you told your dad. Why did you do it? We agreed to keep quiet about it for a reason. You could at least have told me you were thinking of saying something. I'm really not happy about this. Who else have you told?

To: Ruth
From: Lewis
Subject: Re: Your e-mail

Don't know how this happened. I'm sure I didn't do this by mistake. Anyway, sorry. Of course nothing excuses what happened. But there's a difference between what I really think and what I want my dad to think. Do you understand what I mean? I know nothing makes up for it. I'm sorry if I hurt you by telling him. I haven't told anyone else.
Lewis

I suspected Ruth would be keen to keep whatever Lewis did to her a secret. Protecting him, no doubt. My stomach's all knotted. I should do something. But what? At least Lewis blames himself for sending

Ruth the e-mail. I should be OK to push things a bit further without him realising.

A piercing scream rips through my head. What's *that*? Oh no, the smoke alarm. Damn – my toast.

7 June 2001   1:09am

I just about managed to avert disaster last night. Everyone came to have a moan at me, but that was a small price to pay for coming across as a normal – if careless – guy who just happened to be having a midnight snack. It's ironic that I'm so careful to stay unnoticed but I'm almost sunk by a slice of blackened bread. I'm going to have to rethink my late-night diet. Maybe cereal is the way forward.

I saw something strange as I walked past the yard this evening. There was a lad hanging around – late teens, looked like one of the ones they chucked out after the first round of *Popstars* – talking to Lewis as he locked the gates. Lewis isn't one to make idle conversation with strangers, and I got the impression that he wished it wasn't happening. I don't think he was just some yob giving Lewis a bit of hassle. The lad seemed confident, like he was there for a reason. I was dying to walk extra slowly, but as there was no one else around, I'd have stood out a mile. I check to see who else Lewis has been talking to. There are two new messages:

To: Readyloan.com
From: Lewis
Subject: Application

Dear Sir or Madam
I would like to apply for the Maximiser personal loan as advertised on your website. My application is attached. Assuming it's approved, can you tell me how soon the funds will be in my bank account?
Lewis Richardson

To: Instaloan.co.uk
From: Lewis
Subject: Inquiry

I do not own my home, but I have a 50% share in a successful club.
Can you still consider me for the £5,000 homeowner loan? Please
could you e-mail me ASAP.
Lewis Richardson

His urgency speaks for itself. But how does this desperation for cash
fit with his offer to buy Finn's half of the Loft? Yet again, the trail's
gone cold. I go to Lisa's e-mail. She's sent that questionnaire thing
to Kim.

What time is it?	1:40am
Name as it appears on your birth certificate:	Lisa Jane Hunter
Nickname at school:	Then: Lise. Now: Haven't got one
Pets:	None
Piercings:	Ears (wow)
Tattoos:	Want little bird on my shoulder and Celtic band on my arm
Been to how many continents?	Two
Dumper or dumpee?	Neither yet
Favourite place to be kissed:	Wherever
Talker or listener?	Listener (no one listens to me, so what choice have I got?)
Most annoying trait in others:	Judging me before they know me
Fantasy partner:	Joaquin Phoenix
Most embarrassing incident:	Being at Hollyoaks Comprehensive (one big continuous embarrassment)

Fighter or lover:	Am both, need chance to prove it
Favourite position:	Yeah, right
Proudest moment:	None. Got a lot of catching up to do
Favourite word:	Safe
Biggest fear:	Obvious, so 'pass'
Loved somebody so much it made you cry?	(Duh…) Yes
If yes, who?	Obvious, so 'pass' (thanks for sending me this, Kim!!)

To: Kim
From: Lisa
Subject: Facts of life

Sorry about you and Jason. I did wonder if there was something between him and Sarah after James King's party. Maybe I should have told you but you'd only have worried, and at least you know the truth now. (Sorry, that sounds really cold. If I was there, I'd give you a big hug.) Maybe this isn't the best time to tell you we had a PSE lesson today. It was hilarious. It was with Miss Jennings, this ultra-square biology teacher who wears sandals and looks like she cuts her own hair (with a knife and fork, according to Abby). She got off to a bad start when she started talking about the vulva and this lad, Jon Pugh, said, 'My mum's got one. It's a really smooth ride.' Everyone went silent, Miss J looked up all outraged and went 'What?' and Jon said, 'A Volvo, Miss.' She should have chucked him out really, but she just looked embarrassed, like she was dying to laugh but was too scared. She had this big box on the desk and she kept taking out her 'visual aids' one by one. She went through loads of boring stuff about the Pill, but the best bit was when she brought out this gross, rubbery (the colour of earwax, mmm, tempting) plastic willy. (All the lads were saying how come the school couldn't afford a full-size one, chortle chortle.) Miss J was really nervous about saying the word 'penis' because she sort of started, then coughed in the middle, so the second bit came out all high pitched and squeaky and loud, like 'pe-*eenis*!' She went bright red, and I was giggling so much I thought I was going to throw up. Anyway,

she opened a condom and sort of yanked it onto the earwax knob. (If I was the bloke I don't think I'd need it any more by this point, but whatever.) Then Jonny said, really quietly, 'Now let's see you do it no hands.' and the whole back row just creased up. Zara, Abby and Steph reckon she's a lesbian (but then again, I reckon every girl must have seen the advantages after looking at that mutant willy-thing). Actually I think she's just a virgin. Well, they say it takes one to know one… Afterwards, we were all laughing about it and I was like yeah, maybe I have got some mates after all. Zara reckoned she was going to use the free condoms with Brian. Well, I'll soon find out. I'm starting to get the hang of this gossip business…
Lisa

To: Zara
From: Lisa
Subject: Did you?!

Hi Za, what's happening? Yes, I *am* trying to ask whether you and Brian 'took things further', but can you blame me after the way you dragged him off? *Well*?
Lisa

To: Lisa
From: Zara
Subject: Re: Did you?!

No, we didn't do it but something much, much better happened ☺. We got close, but then he pulled away like he usually does, and I said what's wrong. He said he doesn't think a couple should do it unless they're really in love. Then he said there was a problem, and I'm like, oh my God, this is it, I'm so gonna get dumped. But he said the problem is that he thinks he loves me!! I feel amazing, I'm so happy ☺☺!! I really, really love him and I know this was his way of saying he's going to be ready for us to do it soon. It's really stupid, but I wanted to do it cos I thought that way I wouldn't lose him. I'm not in a rush any more because I know he's serious about me and that's what really matters… Don't tell Abby and Steph, will you, cos I want to see their faces when I tell them!!!
Za

I feel like I've intruded on something private here and I get a belated pang of conscience. Better move on to someone with a tougher skin – I can't stand feeling guilty.

To: Izzy
From: Geri
Subject: Get over it

If Alex has decided he's had enough of being bossed around by an overgrown ego in Nikes, he has every right to join my team. I've heard you were shouting at Anna about this earlier today. Please note that: (a) Alex has a mind of his own and has made his decision, (b) Anna is my friend and you have no right to bully her, and (c) who died and made you queen? You don't get to lay down the law to anyone you don't like the look of, just because you're team captain. Why don't you at least pretend that Game 4 IT is a little less about you and a little more about helping students?
Geri

To: Geri
From: Izzy
Subject: Re: Get over it

Oh please, I've just eaten. And incidentally, your merry band can't be as loyal as you seem to think, because I know all about your little 'dirty tricks' pep talk. You realise the judges will disqualify anyone who's unable to play fair? Just thought I'd remind you, because it'd be terribly embarrassing, not just for you but for the college. And of course it'll all be caught on camera. Perhaps you should have thought of that before turning yourself into head cheerleader for Adam Morgan.
Izzy

To: Anna
From: Geri
Subject: Tomorrow

Aaargh!! *How* much do I want to throttle her with her itty-bitty little cardigan, she whose name I can't even bear to mention? Can you believe she's still trying to make out I'm still controlled by my desire for Adam?

Don't want to scare you, but my team will be out for blood tomorrow. If I don't deliver that girl the biggest ass-whupping of her pampered existence then shoot me, because my life won't be worth living.

Anyway, we both know that isn't the reason I'm writing this. You snapped at me and maybe I deserved it, but that doesn't stop me being concerned about you. I know something's not right. If you're not telling me because you think we're not friends, then this is to say we've officially made up, OK?
Geri

Still desperate to get into the Law of the Stag file, but can't crack the password. I think I just heard a voice outside my door. Got to go.

13 June 2001   12:05am

Just got back from the riverside. The after-event party for Game 4 IT was starting to wind down. I saw Lewis leave with Geri. Interesting and unexpected. If anything, I'd have put my money on Ruth and Lewis having an old-time's-sake moment, because there was definitely something between them earlier in the day. There was no sign of Finn, although I'd heard he was supposed to be taking part. I check Lewis's mail.

To: Finn
From: Lewis
Subject: You

Where are you? Do you think you can just desert the club because you're feeling sorry for yourself? I'm not going to apologise, because I never asked to see you and that girl. Where would it have got us if I'd said nothing? In the same position in six months' time, after six months of me having to lie for you. I'm sorry things have turned out like this, but take a look in the mirror before you blame me.
Lewis

I try Mandy.

To: Cindy
From: Mandy
Subject: Ben

Hope everyone's OK. I thought I'd e-mail you because I've got no chance of getting anything else done. College has gone totally insane with the student games. I'm supposed to be helping make giant stir-fry vegetables (don't ask) and collecting two sumo-wrestling suits (ditto). The other reason I can't concentrate is Ben. I'm really worried about him. Yesterday he spent nearly all day in front of the telly. He won't talk about the fire and he's refusing to have counselling. He seems to be retreating into himself and there's nothing I can do. Things between him and Luke are worse than ever, too. I thought Luke of all people would understand that it takes time to get over a trauma. But they had a massive row yesterday about who's suffered the most. (I know, it'd be almost funny if I didn't have to live through it.) Being stuck in Luke's flat with Laura (who always stays spookily silent whenever there's any trouble) isn't helping. What I really want to do is get away from everyone and let them all sort it out. Totally selfish and unfair on Ben, I know. But your invitation's more tempting than ever – shame I've got no money or time.
Love
Mandy

To: Mandy
From: Ben
Subject: (No subject)

I feel daft e-mailing you when I'm going to see you tonight, but here goes. I wanted to write this down because I've tried to say it but it's not that easy. Sorry if you think I've pushed you away. If I'm going to get over this, I have to do it myself. I know this must be frustrating and I'm sorry, Mand, but if I can't trust myself every time I go into a fire, I've got no right to do the job. Hope you understand this. See you later.
Love
Ben

I go to Finn's e-mail to see if there are any clues about him and Victoria.

> To: Finn
> From: Ruth
> Subject: Want to talk?
>
> You're sitting in the flat, beating yourself up about Victoria. Don't,
> Finn. After what happened with the bricks, she's bound to want
> some time and space to clear her head. It's no reflection on you. I'm
> in this evening if you want a chat.
> Ruth

OK, so those two obviously *aren't* having an affair. I'm surprised he hasn't even told her the truth, though. I find this reply, sent earlier this evening:

> To: Ruth
> From: Finn
> Subject: Re: Want to talk?
>
> Not really in the mood for talking but thanks. You're being way too
> kind to me.
> Finn

A few minutes later, he sent this:

> To: Carol
> From: Finn
> Subject: Last laugh, you can have the
>
> I'm sitting at home with my last can of beer, and I'm trying to
> remember all the times you warned me about myself and told me I
> wasn't worthy of a relationship. There's a lot to remember.
>   I can see you sitting there, laptop, deck, cool drink, gorgeous
> people, sunset. Well, I might just have the final touch to make your
> perfect day even more special. Vicky's walked out. As in, gone,
> because I didn't appreciate what I had and, like you probably told
> me a few hundred times, once you stop appreciating, you start
> screwing up. Well, guess what I've done, big time.

That's the can finished. OK. So now I'm a club owner with no alcohol, and a husband with no wife. You teased me all along about my domestic bliss. Well, you obviously know me a lot better than I know myself. God, Carol, I've been so stupid. I've never felt so alone in my life. Tell me she's going to come back.
Finn

I send this to Ruth. Can't wait to find out what she makes of it.

To: Finn
From: Carol
Subject: Re: Last laugh, you can have the

I'm not laughing. I don't know why you're telling me this or what you expect me to say. Finn, I'm sure she's just gone home to her mum's or wherever, and she'll be back in a day or two. (Isn't it great how the written word masks total insincerity?) Sorry, that was cold. But I'm leaving it in to show you how I feel about your e-mail. I resent the suggestion that I've been waiting for this to happen and that I'm now dancing a jig of glee. I said I wanted you to have a happy life and I don't know why you think I was lying. (If I was there, I'd be running to the offy for you and you know it.)
Carol
PS What does Tony make of it all? Do you suddenly have a lot more empty space in the trouser department? (NB I'm *not* enjoying this.)
PPS You're after my sympathy and you don't have to pretend you're not. But I'm holding back until you fill in the small missing detail, i.e. what you did.

To: Carol
From: Finn
Subject: Re: Last laugh, you can have the

I cheated. Don't ask who because you don't know her – in fact, that makes two of us. Yes, it was that meaningless, and I can see the look on your face because once again I've lived down to your expectations, haven't I? Tony doesn't know what's happened, and neither does Ruth, despite the fact that I've just been crying on

her cyber-shoulder (thank God for e-mail, friend to low-down, lying scum) and I'd be grateful if you'd help to keep it that way.
Finn

I try Adam's mail, in case he's heard anything via Deva.

To: Beth
From: Adam
Subject: All right sis

What's new? How did the date go with Gerard? You two carrying on like the stuff I used to watch in my French cinema phase? Don't be ordering the wedding dress just yet though this time, hey? Ignore me, just being jealous because Mum and Dad and I are now all members of the Single and Desperate Morgan Club. That's not really fair on them, to be honest, because they seem a lot happier now they've decided to go through with the divorce. Zara has decided it's now true love with the only black-lipsticked Christian in captivity, and Luke's shacked up with smiley Laura. Yes, she's letting her sunny personality shine into his gloomy, bachelor lifestyle and I don't think he's too happy about it (like he's got the guts to say anything). Anyway, talking of intrusive behaviour, I might be looking to crash on your floor soon. (Got any fit, Juliette Binoche looky-likey mates who are up for a bit of *le rosbif*? Looks like I've totally run out of sex credits as far as British women go.)
Laters
Ad

Then there's a message he wrote just a couple of hours ago:

To: Kerri
From: Adam
Subject: Hammered

Wotcha babe
Where are you – some amazing island somewhere? Torture me. I'm at home and hammered, so I apologise in advance for wasting your time with incoherent rambling. Mad day. My head's buzzing with it all, so that's why I'm here with you. Just got back from

filming the student games. I kept thinking how you'd have loved it.
Loads of fighting, drinking and running around in wet T-shirts.
Number One and Number Two (as you put it) were dressed as dogs
(!) and had to knock each other off these pillars into a pond.
Number One (getting confused – Geri, right?) won. Afterwards,
things turned ugly – not easy with those two. (Sorry, but I think of
you as one of the lads – in the sexiest possible way of course.)
Hissy fits all round with hair-pulling, etc. Only shame was that it
wasn't over me. The thing was that I was getting the whole day on
tape, and Izzy got massively angry, like I was trying to show her up
or something. God, don't know if I should say this... Let's just say
that it cleared up a few of my feelings about One and Two. Enough
already.
Adam

To: Adam
From: Kerri
Subject: Re: Hammered

Noooooo way! You can't just leave it like that! You are such a tease!
Kerri
PS The two Aussies, three Singaporeans, one Japanese and one
Kiwi reading this with me in Phuket will personally come round
and do you some damage if you don't give us the next instalment
pronto. (Don't go all shy on us, it's not like they know you!)

To: Kerri
From: Adam
Subject: Re: Hammered

What the hell. (Hi, Gossip Nation.) What I'm trying to say is you
were right. I'm not over Izzy. I'm *so* not over her that this little voice
in my head kept going 'what is wrong with you, you don't do
emotional involvement, you're Adam Morgan for God's sake!' I
wish. Anyway, I had a big drink and then an even bigger drink, and I
think I've worked it out. Here's my Theory of Me: I've always gone
for girls who don't really need me. Like you. Come on, admit it. If
it's not in your backpack you can live without it. That was always the
deal with us, wasn't it? Geri's kind of the same. Out for a good time

and nothing more. And you both gave me as many second chances as I wanted. Izzy's different. I saw her all angry today and it all became clear. She won't give me a second chance because I hurt her so badly, and she's still hurting. I think that's what I'm crazy about, the fact that I mattered so much to her and I never realised it until it was too late. Only maybe – please God – it's not, because no one's ever got to me like this before. I don't know whether it's love, infatuation or just screaming lust. Probably all three. All I know is that I want to live up to what she first thought of me when we met. She had faith in me then, and I want to show her that she was right to have it. (Remember I never cheated on her, it was just that stupid film project.) I don't know – am I hoping for too much here? Well, whatever.

Adam

To: Adam
From: Kerri
Subject: Re: Hammered

Go Adam, you let it all out!! The Singapore contingent thinks you should tell her your true feelings, the Aussies are all for a big, romantic gesture and the Kiwi thinks you should 'get the hell over it'. Hiroko from Osaka is sniffling into her Hello Kitty scarf. As for this Aussie, I'm not sure. (Perhaps we could continue this somewhere more private, some time less hammered?)

Kerri

PS Don't mind you thinking of me as tough-as-crocodile-boots backpack chick, but for the record, I did have 'issues' when we split.

Brilliant. I'm desperate to send Adam's e-mail to 'Number Two' herself. Too risky? No, I can't miss out on this – off it goes. I love that assessment of Geri as 'out for a good time and nothing more'. Though to be fair to Adam, that's exactly what I thought of her before I started reading her mail.

I enter Izzy's account to see if Adam's feelings are mutual. I find this, written an hour or so ago.

To: Sis-sis
From: Izzy
Subject: Today

Got to tell you this or I'll EXPLODE. I feel like I've had my guts pulled out and stamped on in public. We lost, by the way, by one lousy point, thanks to Geri (who else?). I didn't really mind who won, as long as it was the best team, but her side *so* didn't deserve it. As if that wasn't enough, she turned on me at the after-games party for daring to put my team through a proper training programme. Then she showed her true colours and called me (very originally) a 'stuck-up little tart'. Drinks were thrown (I couldn't let her get away with calling me that). And wouldn't you know it, all the way through Adam stood there gawping, hoping we'd get stuck into some male-fantasy wrestling sequence. (Geri, of course, would have been only too happy to oblige.) As usual, he was just one step away from cheering her on. I just wish they'd get over themselves and slither off into bed, instead of staging Flirtstock whenever they come within a mile of each other.

    Arrrrgh!!! How much do I hate this place? Actually, I've cheered up a bit now because I've just thought about how I'm going to 'congratulate' her. (One of Uncle Toby's famous sayings!!) Give my hugs to Mummy and Boo-Boo when you see them.

Iz

To: Geri
From: Izzy
Subject: Congratulations

Just goes to prove it's true what they say. Even a blind pig can stumble upon the occasional tasty acorn.

    Well, savour it while it lasts.

Izzy

Can't wait for tomorrow – so much to check up on.

14 June 2001   2:15am

No contest tonight – straight to Finn to see if Ruth has found his e-mail to Carol. Bingo.

> To: Finn
> From: Ruth
> Subject: Re: Last laugh, you can have the
>
> Finn, an e-mail you wrote to Carol has just arrived in my inbox.
> Yesterday, I got one from Lewis to his dad. What's going on? Was
> this a genuine mistake or is someone tampering with your
> account?
>   I know I shouldn't have read it, but it's too late. Why are you
> putting so much blame on yourself? Is there something you haven't
> told me?
> Ruth

I feel shivery, half-scared, half-thrilled. It's the first time since the Zara incident that anyone has suggested 'someone' could be up to no good.

> To: Ruth
> From: Finn
> Subject: Re: Last laugh, you can have the
>
> Sorry about that. I was hitting the beers a bit too hard. Must have
> been feeling a bit sorry for myself. Hence the 'it's all my fault' stuff.
> And you know how Carol likes a good sob story. See you.
> Finn

Nicely wriggled out of, Finn.

> To: Izzy
> From: Geri
> Subject: Re: Congratulations
>
> Dear Izzy

Thank you so much for your kind words! I've passed them on to the rest of my team so they can show their appreciation. We've always known you were a loser; now we know exactly what sort of loser you are. (Were we a little 'tiddly' when we sent that e-mail?)
Cheers!
Geri

To: Lewis
From: Geri
Subject: Last night

OK, so you've probably had about enough of me over the past twenty-four hours. I just wanted to say thanks again for getting me home last night. And, even more importantly, for being a gentleman when we got there. There aren't many of you about. (Actually, I don't think it's physically possible that you put a dry shirt on me with your eyes closed, but thanks for being dishonest.)
I owe you one.
Geri

To: Ruth
From: Geri
Subject: Lewis

Hi Ruth
I know I only spoke to you twenty minutes ago but this is nagging away at me. Maybe it's just hangover paranoia, but I'm sensing that you're not as OK about what happened last night with Lewis as you made out. If I'm right, I totally understand and I apologise. Please be honest. Our friendship is important to me and I don't want anything or anyone to spoil it.
Geri

To: Geri
From: Ruth
Subject: Re: Lewis

Geri, don't be silly. If it bothered me, I'd let you know.
Ruth

To: Anna
From: Geri
Subject: You

How are you? If you want me to come round later, just say. I can't
believe you've been keeping your pregnancy to yourself, Anna. I
knew something wasn't right, and I'm kicking myself because I've
let things between us fester for way too long. I know it's probably
too soon for you to start thinking about what you're going to do,
but I meant what I said, we'll see this through together. If you
want me to, I'll get Alex by the scruff of his neck (or somewhere
more sensitive) and force him to face up to what he's done. Just
say the word.

Since you've opened up to me, I guess it's my turn to 'share'.
What I didn't say earlier (your news was *slightly* more important) is
that Lewis took me home last night. He put me in some dry clothes
and put me to bed. No, nothing happened (although I didn't find that
out until I spoke to him). Can't face going through the whole gory
tale, so here's a summary of my thoughts today:
1. What am I doing in this top?
2. *Who* was I doing in this top?
3. Oh no, Lewis.
4. Oh no, *Ruth*.
5. Phew, nothing happened.
6. (*Why* didn't anything happen?) (Only kidding...)
7. Lewis, what a nice guy.
8. Oh no, *Ruth*.
9. Lewis, what a nice guy.
10. Oh no, *Ruth*.
7, 8, 9 and 10 are the thoughts currently chasing each other round
in my head. I can't believe Ruth's as cool about this as she makes
out. So the sensible thing would be to shut the door on the whole
incident, because I really don't want to upset her (she's sort of
become a substitute Anna since we 'lost touch'). But I also want to
take Lewis out for a drink, (a) for not behaving like 99% of the male
population, and (b) because I like him. That's 'like' as in, I'd like to
spend time with him (and, I suppose, as in 'see what happens'...).
Anyway, I was watching Lewis at the games. He didn't take his eyes
off Ruth all day, so maybe I'm just being me here. Be honest

though, Anna. If I followed my instincts, how badly would I be
betraying Ruth on a scale of one to ten?
Geri
PS Apparently Ruth brought John Stuart home last night!! Did *you*
know there was anything going on?

This just has to go to Ruth.

To: Geri
From: Anna
Subject: Re: You

I don't know, two, maybe three. It wouldn't really be betrayal
because they've split up, but I can see how she might not be thrilled
about it.
     Thanks for all the stuff you said about me being pregnant.
You've already helped me loads. I cried when I read your e-mail. I
think it's because Alex should have been saying all this, not you.
Don't want you to confront him, though. If he's going to do anything,
it has to be because he wants to, otherwise I don't want to know.
Anna

To: Geri
From: Lewis
Subject: Re: Last night

No problem. Not sure how to take all this gratitude though. All I did
was take you home (because you didn't know who or where you
were, and I didn't want you sleeping at the bottom of the River Dee),
change your wet top (to stop you getting pneumonia) and fail to try
anything on with you (to avoid being a total, lowlife scumbag).
Which part of this comes as a surprise exactly? You can tell me
over a pint in the Dog. Can't make it for a day or two, though.
Overworked and exhausted, you know how it is. (Of course you do,
you're a student.) (Sorry.)
Lewis

I go to Lewis's mail. In the hour or so after the e-mail to Geri, he sent
off five applications and three enquiries to online loan companies.

For the first time in a while, I can't help feeling a bit sorry for him. Underneath all the desperate attempts to be funny, he must have meant what he said about being exhausted. For the first time, I start to feel we have something in common.

Nearly forgot – Adam's declaration of love for Izzy. I check Izzy's e-mail. It's there, but she hasn't responded.

15 June 2001   1:20am

I've had a worrying day. I made a couple of mistakes as a result of being sleep-deprived. Geri and Ruth both noticed that my personal grooming wasn't up to usual standards. I gave them the huge workload excuse, but I can't get away with that forever. The truth is, my snooping sessions have been getting longer because I've got involved in so many people's lives. 'I want to know' has become 'I've got to know', and I don't see any way back.

To: Izzy
From: Chloe
Subject: Acorn

Dear Izzy
Thanks for your heartfelt message of congratulation to our team captain. Here's mine: YOU LOST! Now I'll return to our celebrations. We're all here knocking back a few buckets of swill and rolling around in a fifty-fifty blend of mud and our own pooh. We may reek, but the smell of victory is sweet.
Chloe

To: Izzy
From: Luke
Subject: Blind pig

Oink, grunt, snuffle, snort.
Luke

To: Izzy
From: Andy Morgan
Subject: Pig

No hard feelings. Come into Deva today and have one of our new specials, on the house – the four-rasher bacon, lettuce and tomato baguette we've christened the 'Izzy'.
Andy

To: Sis-sis
From: Izzy
Subject: Games

Delete that last one *please*, your baby sis was rather tired and very emotional. I'm no longer stewing in self-pity. I've realised that if the games prove anything, it's how pathetically needy Geri is. She's spent the last couple of days walking around telling everyone who'll listen what a 'loser' I am. If she didn't have other people's approval, she'd shrivel up and die. Adam, as I predicted, is being his usual immature self about the film. I'm pretty sure this is part of his strategy to keep in with Geri, just in case no one better (or more available) comes along. Anyway, who cares? At least I can concentrate on the play again. It's starting to take shape now. Remember I told you about Max? He's so much better than I thought he'd be. He doesn't know what he's doing half the time, and his technique's pretty rough, but he puts so much energy into it when he gets going that it's quite exciting. He's quite a geeky-looking lad really, but he's got quite a lot of passion inside him and I'm doing whatever I can to bring it out.
Love and hugs
Iz

That's one for O.B. to enjoy tomorrow.

To: Adam
From: Izzy
Subject: Your film

Members of my team tell me that your 'editing' sessions on the Game 4 IT film principally involve action replays of the bit where I

was knocked into the water, shown to an ever-decreasing audience (Matt and O.B. at the last count). Adam, don't you think you're being a little bit sad and immature? Though I appreciate that there *is* something very fitting about this – you going over and over the past, me moving on. But if I were you, I'd do it in the privacy of my own room. The little respect you have in this college is running out fast.
Iz

To: Izzy
From: Adam
Subject: Re: Your film

Ouch, Iz, that one stung! Hmm, immature and sad – you've never called me *that* before. (What's that you were saying about moving on?) All I did was film what happened. If I get pleasure out of repeated viewing, where's the harm? You know what I think? You enjoy sending me these lectures. You like to think you've given me a good telling-off, don't you? Izzy, we were all there to have fun. If you'd taken yourself a bit less seriously and gone with the spirit of it, who knows, you might even have had a good time. You used to have a sense of humour, don't tell me you've ditched it just to win people's 'respect.' Deep down, you're smart and funny and better than that, and you're going to start making me feel nostalgic for the old days. If I'm doing something that's bothering you, why don't you say so to my face and we'll sort it out?
Ad

No reply from Izzy. I go to Adam's mail.

To: Kerri
From: Adam
Subject: no no no no NO

Aarrgh! I've screwed up. Got a snotty e-mail from Izzy about the film I made, complaining that I was making fun of her (basically true, though she doesn't realise *why*). Any sane person in my position would have gone to see her, apologised, grovelled, etc. What did I do? Slip on my bed-me jeans and head round to her room with a bunch of whatever? No, but hey, I did something almost as seductive: I sent her an equally snotty e-mail. I've just read it again and it makes me cringe. Guaranteed to remind her what a sarky, patronising bundle of sexual frustration she's missing out on. Anyway, by now you've probably worked out that my problem is fear of rejection. Well, Ms Freud, it's worse than that. I've joked and bantered and told myself I don't care for so long, I'm now completely incapable of putting myself in the firing line. Why don't you consult the United Nations again and tell me what I should do.

Adam

To: Adam
From: Kerri
Subject: Re: no no no no NO

Adam, Adam, calm yourself down boy! No United Nations today as I'm on my own (in an internet café in Phnom Penh, Cambodia, but I know your inner turmoil makes these little details seem irrelevant). I think I can work this one out for myself. You go and see her. You buy her a coffee or similar beverage. You say sorry. You repeat as necessary until you get a 'result'. You e-mail Kerri, who kicks herself black and blue because she's just destroyed her chances with her favourite Brit (though hopefully he'll let her crash on the floor/share the children's room in the future Adam 'n' Posh Girl love-nest).

Kerri

PS You know that stuff you were telling me about Luke pining for Mandy, then watching her go off with someone else? Are you sure you're not holding back from Izzy because you're scared the same thing's going to happen to you?

There's just time for a quick check of Geri's e-mail before I log off.

To: Geri
From: Ruth
Subject: Your e-mail

Hi

Just in case you get this before you come home… I got an e-mail from you yesterday that was meant for Anna. Anyway, I've deleted

it. I'm a bit worried about this – it's the third time it's happened now.
Have you had any problems?
Ruth
PS OK, I did read it, I'm only human. The only thing that bothers me
is your suggestion that John Stuart spent the night. I told you he
didn't and I'm really surprised that you've decided to spread it.

To: Anna
From: Geri
Subject: Oh my God

Oh my God, you won't believe what I've done. Somehow that e-mail
about Lewis got sent to *Ruth*. There's no way I'd have done that by
accident. Is there some way it can just happen, a virus or
something? This is where Alex would be handy. (Sorry, not the
most sensitive thing to say, but you know what I mean.) Like things
weren't embarrassing enough already.
Geri

Uh-oh, doing three hits on the same person wasn't the wisest move.
Better call it a night.

18 June 2001   1:54am

Plenty of mail for Lewis today, nearly all of it from loan companies.
Four rejections and three acceptances, subject to further checks. But
there's still nothing to suggest a reason why he needs this money.
This looks interesting, though:

To: Lewis
From: Ruth
Subject: Geri

Geri still seems really worried about the other night. Maybe she's
reading too much into what happened, but she's concerned that
she's offended me. If you speak to her, can you just tell her to relax?

I've told her that we're finished but she doesn't seem to believe me 100%.
Ruth

What's this, Saint Ruth delivering a cleverly subtle attack on Geri and Lewis? In three sentences, she's managed to puncture Geri's aura of cool and suggest to Lewis that she isn't bothered what they get up to. That e-mail from Geri has definitely got her back up.

To: Finn
From: Ruth
Subject: Where are you?

Hi Finn
What's up? I haven't seen you around for days. Lewis mentioned something about you having 'flu. Is this about Victoria? I assume she's still away. Finn, you can't underestimate what's happened to her. It's not like she's rejecting you, and it's no reason for you to shut yourself away. Anyway, she'll be back soon. (If she's still set on having a baby she'll want to get practising.) Give me a call or something.
Ruth

To: Ruth
From: Finn
Subject: Re: Where are you?

All right Ruth?
I know, I know, you're right as always. Just been feeling a bit under the weather. The Vicky thing hasn't helped, but relax, there's no moping or anything of that sort going down over here.
Finn

To: Finn
From: Tony
Subject: Morning!

Hi Finn
Never thought I'd say this, but I think you've made the right decision, standing up to Mum re. the baby issue. I'm sure she'll

come to realise it was just a reaction to the near-miss. You need to woo her again. Make her feel special. Learn to cook the food she likes (desserts can work wonders). I'm at your disposal if you need any advice.
Tony

To: Tony
From: Finn
Subject: Re: Morning!

Cheers for the advice, Tone. Don't want to rush things though. I've got to give her time to reach her own decision.
Finn

I never realised someone could be that laid back *and* a good liar. Not that he's told many lies – he's just left blanks and waited for other people to fill them in.

Right – where next?

To: Zara
From: Steph
Subject: Blind date

Hi! How did it go with that woman and your dad? What was she like? Abby said she looked too old to be your step-mum. Do you reckon they're going to see each other again?
Steph

To: Steph
From: Zara
Subject: Re: Blind date

No, Dad didn't fancy her. He's only looking for a girlfriend, anyway – he doesn't want to settle down again. I don't care what she's like as long as she knows how to splash the ca$h!! Can't wait till they get divorced properly. Should be a laugh playing them off against each other when it's my birthday, etc. Plus when Mum has a boyfriend to go out with, I'll be able to have Brian round whenever I want without anyone there to moan at me, cool or what?
Za

To: Lisa
From: Zara
Subject: Hi

Hi Lisa
Sorry I was a bit off with you at break-time. I just feel weird about
everything at the moment. Steph and Abby keep going on about
Dad's blind date, like I needed reminding. Everyone thinks all I care
about is who I get as a step-mum, but it's not. I think Dad might be
depressed. He looked so sad when he came into Deva after the
date. I think he might have wanted to see her again but she said no
or something. This whole divorce thing is doing my head in. Mum
keeps asking me what's wrong and I want to say to her, what do
you think? Our whole family is just this massive mistake that
happened because they got married when they shouldn't have. Dad
keeps saying we have to look forward now, oh yeah, to more dates
where he ends up like a sad, old man at the end of the night?
I don't know why I'm telling you this really. Probably cos I don't
know why I can't have a normal family like yours.
Za

To: Kim
From: Lisa
Subject: Normal

How are you? I had to send you this, from Zara. Just wanted to
show you how far your best mate has come. 'I don't know why I
can't have a normal family like yours.' Can you believe I'm that
convincing?
Lisa
(Attachment: Hi)

I knew I was right about her family.

I've got to see if anything's come of that Izzy message I sent to O.B.

To: Adam, Geri, Chloe, Jonno, Marley, Paul, Jez, Josh, Sprout, Wilco, Taylor
From: O.B.
Subject: Max's secret love

So now we know what kind of 'performance' got Max the part! Respect!

Remember I told you about Max? He's so much better than I thought he'd be. He doesn't know what he's doing half the time, and his technique's pretty rough, but he puts so much energy into it when he gets going that it's quite exciting. He's quite a geeky-looking lad really, but he's got quite a lot of passion inside him and I'm doing whatever I can to bring it out.
Love and hugs
Iz

What is he *on?* This is not what I need. I had no idea O.B. was going to cut a chunk from Izzy's e-mail and make it sound like an assessment of Max's bedroom skills. It's bound to get back to Izzy sooner or later.

To: Adam, O.B., Ruth, Izzy, Anna, Chloe, Matt, Taylor, Mandy
From: Geri
Subject: E-mail problems

Hi. Just wondered if anyone else has been having problems with their e-mails. There have been several times over the past few weeks when I've received e-mails intended for other people, or my e-mails have been sent where they shouldn't have been. Is this just me? If you've had anything like this happen, please let me know. Thanks.
Geri

A bit unsettling, I admit, but there've been plenty of scares like this before and no one's even thought about investigating. I'll just be careful when I involve Geri from now on.

To: O.B.
From: Max
Subject: Your e-mail

Did you spend time making that up or what? If not, did you hack into Izzy's e-mail just to dig for dirt on me? You jealous git! She's going to freak when she sees this (which she will, like right now).
Max

To: Max
From: O.B.
Subject: Re: Your e-mail

Calm down! I never hacked into anything, she sent it to me by accident. Anyway, what's the problem if people think you two have got it on?
O.B.
PS Forgotten the password to Stag File.

Got to find out whether Max has been in touch with Izzy about this.

To: Izzy
From: Max
Subject: E-mail

Hi Izzy
I know you must be really hacked off about the e-mail that's going round. It's just O.B. being Mr Maturity as usual. He claims it got sent to him 'by accident'. I don't want to drop him in it, as he is supposed to be my mate. Just thought you should know.
Max

To: O.B.
From: Izzy
Subject: 'Max's secret love'

Almost as hilarious as the e-mail to Max that 'accidentally' found its way to me. Where did you get this from?? You better give me an honest answer unless you actually *want* it to be on the principal's desk first thing tomorrow.
Izzy

To: O.B.
From: Max
Subject: Re: Your e-mail

Been in touch then has she? Shot yourself in the foot there, didn't
you mate? Never mind, I'm sure you haven't blown your chances,
what with her being, you know, well into you and everything! (What
do you want to go into the stag stuff for, you tosser?)
Max

Ah Max, almost cunning but not quite. Once I've banged out the
password – *tosser* – I'm straight into the encrypted file, now
handily decrypted. *Yes*!! At last I can find out what went on.

Remember!! All information in this file is governed by the Law of
the Stag. Disclosure to non-Stags = Death (slowly)
All right lads, keep it clean, we all got up to stuff we don't want to
boast about so let's not try to embarrass each other!! So, O.B.,
what's it like to snog a bloke? – Max
What's this? (PS Is anyone else still suffering the effects of dodgy
sangria? My bumhole's twitching like a mouse's ear.) – Finn
You serious? No way! – Ben
Oh yeah, tongues, the lot, he's still putting baby lotion on his stubble
burn. – Max
It was a tranny, alright? Anyone could've made the same mistake,
'it' had two inches of slap on. – O.B.
And six inches in his undercrackers. – Max
Classy. Was he better or worse looking than Alex? I hear he got so
into the whole dressing-as-a-woman thing, Geri has to keep her
bras and panties under lock and key. – Ben
You're well pervy, mate. – O.B.
So what was it like taking a walk on the wild side? – Ben
I wouldn't know, cos nothing happened – O.B.
Yeah, right. So how come your lift kept going up and down? – Max
He was pushing the buttons, wasn't he. – O.B.
You said it… – Ben
What about you, anyway? I hear your birds threw up when you tried
to get off with them. – O.B.

You mean Jane and Michelle, who deserted you cos we were more fun? Yeah, they were a bit unwell. They got themselves cleaned up, but they were still pretty dirty if you know what I mean!!! – Ben

You what?! – Luke

You heard. – Ben

No way!! When was this? Was it Jane or Michelle? – Luke

When I went missing in action (told you I was going to the bog but I never said it was the gents, did I?). Let's just say they spared me the awkwardness of having to choose (lucky Jane had breath mints on her). – Ben

Can't believe you. What happened? – Luke

What didn't happen? All I can say is I was locked and loaded, and it would have been rude not to. Still got the scars – M (I think) left her nail marks in my butt. And by the way, the cubicle nearly collapsed onto the *senorita* having a slash next door. – Ben

Class! – Finn

You are a total hound. – Luke

Arf, arf! You can talk!! You so wanted to! Don't try and deny it, cos it was visible mate – we're talking major lumber. – Ben

Sad man. You got wood kissing a stranger with a blindfold on? – Finn

That's complete crap. – Luke

Oh, what? I saw it, plus you told me! I was getting the drinks in and you came over and went 'Timberrr!' Admit it mate, you're double gutted cos I did something about it (by the way, is it true old Tony managed to pot the pink as well?? Miracle!) – Ben

Yeah, once more for old time's sake with Carol. – Max

I don't mind you exchanging banter, but it was not 'for old time's sake.' OK, so we've known each other for a while, but this was the start of a new phase in our relationship, not something seedy and convenient. – Tony

Oooh! Handbags! – Max

Got to have some fun with this. I need to take precautions first. I create a new, free e-mail account for myself and get busy.

To: Izzy, Chloe, Jonno, Marley, Paul, Jez, Josh, Sprout, Wilco
From: Monkey 100
Subject: O.B.

What's the difference between a man's and a woman's idea of foreplay?
You're not alone – O.B. doesn't know either. But remember, 'anyone could have made the same mistake'!

I cut and paste the stuff about O.B. into my e-mail and send it. Then I send the stuff about Ben's antics with Jane and Michelle to Mandy. Time to get out of here.

19 June 2001   1:15am

There are so many things I need to check on tonight. First, I have to see whether anything's been stirred up by Geri's e-mail.

To: Anna
From: Geri
Subject: Lewis

Sorry I didn't meet you for lunch like we arranged. Might come into college later, when I'm not so likely to bump into Ruth. Big news. Lewis stayed last night. God, Anna, what have I got myself into this time?? I was chatting to him outside Deva one minute, and the next I was listening to myself asking him back for dinner. Well, you've guessed it, we had that and more. And now I feel *soooo* weird. Ruth knows what's going on but I haven't psyched myself up to talk to her yet. I've spent the entire day trying to read the same chapter about sexual politics in Spanish cinema, but my mind keeps switching to things closer to home:
(1) I tried to get back with Adam by conspiring with him in his film project. People alienated: Anna, Izzy, Alex, Tony. Success/Failure: Failure.
(2) I had a casual fling with Taylor. People alienated: Ruth (OK, not quite, but I can't believe she was totally cool about it) Success/Failure: Fun while it lasted, but overall, a failure.

(3) I start something with Lewis. People alienated: Ruth.
Success/Failure: Who knows?

Doesn't look good, does it? Why do I always end up scrambling over the people who are closest to me to find a half-decent man? When I see Ruth, I know I'll act all casual but all the time I'll be thinking, if I were you, I'd hate me. The worst thing is that I really, *really* like Lewis. One night together and I'm already starting to get the old Adam feelings for him, except Lewis is so different, in a good way. I've never been with anyone who's so totally focussed on me, who just wants to pay me attention and make me feel good. I sound like a total ego queen I know, but it was soooo sexy. For once it wasn't about a man expecting me to worship at the sacred temple of his manhood, or whatever (mentioning no names, Adam). I felt like Lewis was blanking everything else out – even himself – and I was all that mattered for the whole time we were together. In other words, the complete opposite of everyone else I've been out with. Oh God, listen to me!! He'll probably dump me tomorrow and this'll be evidence of my terminal inability to learn from my mistakes.
Geri

PS You didn't reply about the possible hacker. Have you had any problems?

PPS Had dream about breaking into loads of houses, going through people's valuables and legging it before they woke up. Hmm, *that's* a surprise.

Funny, I'd have thought Lewis had enough complications in his life without sneaking around with Geri in his ex's flat. I'm dying to send this to Ruth, but she and Geri are hyper-alert at the moment. I'll toss a coin. Heads I'll send it, tails I'll be cautious. *Heads*.

To: Geri
From: Anna
Subject: Re: Lewis

At the risk of sounding totally me, are you sure about this? It sounds like all Lewis has done is treat you like a human being. I'm not trying to take away what you feel for him. I just want you to stay aware. Because the way you're talking, you sound as though you've already made your mind up. I suppose I'm just saying you don't know him that well. My other thought is: are you sure you're not just keen *because* of all the stuff with Ruth, forbidden fruit, etc.? This may be totally unfair, but nobody got hurt from being over-cautious, did they?

Don't know why you're asking me, anyway, with the state my relationship is in. Still can't get over Alex admitting he never had a second fertility test. Did he really think he'd 'catch me out' and get me to admit Adam was the father? Please don't go and see him, though.
Anna

To: Anna
From: Geri
Subject: Re: Lewis

OK, bit of a confession. I had a word with Alex. I honestly couldn't stop myself, he was so stubborn. The strange thing was, he was more freaked out when I told him you were going to have the baby (don't know if this is true or not, but I wanted to remind him how real this situation is) than by the whole 'I can't be the father' thing. Seemed to me like he was starting to come round (but don't kill me if it turns out to be wishful thinking).
Geri

Wonder if Ruth's told Finn how she feels about the Geri situation?

To: Ruth
From: Finn
Subject: OK?

Feel weird about how we left things today. I feel crap because I used your shoulder to cry on about Victoria, but I didn't even tell you the truth about why she left. It's a bit late now that you know all the gory details, but anyway – sorry, Ruth.

To: Finn
From: Ruth
Subject: Re: OK?

I'd be lying if I said I wasn't just a bit hurt, but I'm OK about it now. Why did you put yourself through the hassle of not telling me? I've lived with Lewis, it'd take more than that to shock me. Still not sure why you wanted a one-night stand, though. Tell me to butt out if you like, but just think it through before you go making a grand gesture to win her back. It's not my place to say this, but I know things weren't great between you and Victoria before this happened. I'm not saying don't try again, but don't kid yourself that it was all perfect. There was a time when we were close and you used to tell me everything, remember? (But then again, maybe that was part of the problem.)
Ruth

To: Ruth
From: Finn
Subject: Re: OK?

Don't know why I didn't tell you. Well, I sort of do. When you found out Victoria had gone, you assumed it was because of the accident, not something I'd done. You thought the best of me and it felt good. It wasn't a calculated thing, honest. It just felt better being Mr Traumatised-but-Loving Husband than Mr Lowlife Sleep-Around. And I suppose I was scared to tell you in case you booted me out of your sympathy zone, which would have been a disaster (for me at least).

    As for winning her back, you're right. Things weren't always great, but they were a million times better than what I've got now. That bird had it right in that song, about not knowing what you've got till it's gone. Probably sounds corny to you, but to me it's just fact. The one-night stand was me trying to prove I could go back to the old days if I wanted to, but guess what, the bloke I was doesn't exist any more. I resented Vic for trying to change me, but the change happened in me when I fell for her. I just want the chance to tell her that I like how I've changed. Whew! Navel-gazer alert. (There's still hope, isn't there?)

OK... Now you've sorted out my love life, what about yours? Lewis tells me you're getting jiggy with Sir? Details, please.
Finn
PS We are still close, aren't we? Don't really get what you meant by the last bit.

To: Finn
From: Ruth
Subject: Re: OK?

Finn, just tell her what you told me. (I'm convinced, if that counts for anything.)

Re 'Sir' (AKA John Stuart). Still haven't worked out whether it's an admiration thing or a boy-girl thing. I know you're saying 'yeah right', but I'm genuinely confused. As Lewis no doubt told you (so what did he say?), I've given John a couple of chances to let me know what his take on the whole thing is, but he hasn't given much away. (I've just read that last line again. All right, I'll say it before you do: I virtually threw myself at him and he either recoiled in horror or showed admirable self-restraint, depending on whether you listen to Unconfident or Confident Me.) Don't know what to do next because I really like him. Can't talk about this with anyone else (especially not Geri) because there's enough gossip in college as it is. Which is the other thing that makes this a nice, straightforward relationship. Help!!

The other taboo subject is Lewis. He stayed with Geri last night. Can't explain how this makes me feel. (Definitely not jealousy, in case you're wondering.) I'm more fed up with Geri than Lewis. In her defence, she keeps asking me if I'm OK with it, but what am I supposed to say? (I shouldn't *need* to say anything, should I?)

She's convinced herself it's fine to sleep with my ex in my flat, and although it should be, it just so isn't. Technically, she's not doing anything wrong, but in terms of friendship, she's crossed so many lines and she doesn't even seem to realise it. I know I should be cool about this and I even feel guilty for talking about her behind her back like this. Advice, please.
Ruth
PS I was just saying that the time you spent with me you should have been spending with Victoria. I'm not trying to say there was

anything going on that shouldn't have been. But you should've been more comfortable talking to your wife than your friend.

PPS Have you had anything odd happen to your e-mail, break-ins, etc., or is it just a college thing?

To: Ruth
From: Finn
Subject: Re: OK?

So I'm not the only one who's been holding back on the personal details. Like, when did all this start? (Lewis thinks at the Game 4 IT thing, I'm guessing some time before.) Lucky I'm good at reading between the lines. I'll ignore all the 'do I just admire his mind' stuff because you clearly have the screaming hots for this man. I'd go with Confident You. I think he's taking it easy because he doesn't want to go down the quickie-in-the-projector-cupboard route. But if you give him any more chances and he doesn't leap at them (and you), then dump him quick and tell him from me that he's a fool. Don't know what to say about Geri. I see your point, but from my brief encounter with her, I know how her mind works. When you say you're OK with it, I reckon she really believes you, cos she thinks everyone is as straight-talking as she is. So don't be too hard on her, hey? Sorry about this, but I take a selfish view of it all. Anything that helps Lewis straighten out his head and his loins has to make my life easier.

Finn

PS Don't really see what you're getting at. (Am I just being stupid?)

PPS I know the stag file thing has been broken into. Come to think of it, I did send an e-mail to Carol a while back that ended up with Tony. (Yeah, yeah, I know what you're thinking. So us buffoons can now blame our computer screw-ups on a mystery hacker? Excellent!)

To: Finn
From: Ruth
Subject: Re: Lewis

Re your PS, that's not really true, Finn. Not the way I remember it, anyway. I don't see why you're getting defensive just because I've been honest.

To: Ruth
From: Finn
Subject: Re: Lewis

I'm not. I know there was a bit of something between us that could've turned into a big something, and it wouldn't have been a disaster if it had. But things are so crazy with Victoria, etc. (and John Stuart, let's not forget him), that I don't even want to let myself think about it. You know me well enough to know I don't care about you any less for saying this.
Always your mate
Finn

To: Finn
From: Ruth
Subject: Re: Lewis

Yeah, it could've, but we decided not to let it. It's not a big deal, I just didn't want to think you were re-writing history. OK, now we've cleared that one up... See you.
Ruth

I'm going to have to learn to trust my instincts. I *knew* there was something between them, I just jumped to the wrong conclusions. Which is probably what Lewis will do when I send him Finn's 'big something' e-mail...

To: Carol
From: Tony
Subject: Our e-mails

Hi, how are things? Don't be alarmed, but there's a rumour going round that someone's snooping on e-mails. Just thought we should tone things down until they've caught who's doing it. Got to dash.
Love
Tony

To: Tony
From: Carol
Subject: Re: Our e-mails

If we toned them down any more, they'd be blank. Is anyone really
going to want to read your last e-mail about Mr Morgan's wind
problem? (PS The clue is in the question.) Tone, I know there's
passion in there somewhere, I just wish you'd let a bit more of it
into your e-mails, and stuff whatever saddo is listening in. It gets
lonely out here, you know.
Carol

To: Geri
From: Izzy
Subject: Re: E-mail problems

As you know, this has happened to me. Do you think we should get
the guy in IT to look into it?

To: Geri
From: Ruth
Subject: Re: E-mail problems

Yeah. Something's definitely going on. I think we should get the
college to check it out.
Ruth

Right. And do *what*, exactly? This doesn't scare me.

To: Izzy
From: Geri
Subject: Max

OK, I'm in a dilemma here. Half of me wants to congratulate you on
the beautiful thing that you've found with Max, the other half thinks
there've already been too many odd e-mails round here recently.
What's going on?

To: Izzy
From: Adam
Subject: 'Max's secret love'

What's this? Assuming you've seen it and that it's some kind of hoax. Anyway, just thought you should know. Give me a ring if you're worried about it.
Ad

To: Izzy
From: Chloe
Subject: Weird mail

Just a warning that I got something supposedly from you via O.B. Geri mentioned something about weird mail arriving in students' inboxes… Perhaps you should give Mr O'Brien a few, well-chosen words of warning.
Chloe

To: O.B.
From: Izzy
Subject: Warning

I assume you're also 'Monkey 100' who's been sending puerile messages about a stag party. This isn't funny. Half the college is out for your blood. Everyone knows you've been sneaking into loads of students' e-mail accounts. Ruth's minutes away from telling administration.

To: Izzy
From: O.B.
Subject: Re: Warning

The e-mail about you was sent to my inbox from yours. I don't know how it got there. I only passed it on for a bit of fun and I'm sorry if I upset you. I haven't sneaked into anyone's accounts. What's 'Monkey 100', and what stag party?
Sam O'Brien

To: O.B.
From: Jonno
Subject: Tranny

Wa-hey! That's the danger of going for the roughest bird in the room, mate!! Let's hear the details, don't keep us in suspenders...

To: Max
From: O.B.
Subject: You're dead

I'm going to kill you, Cunningham. Why did you send everyone that e-mail about Barcelona? Get some age! Oh, and guess what, everyone thinks I'm a hacker and Ruth's going to report me to the college. Thanks a lot, 'mate'.

To: O.B.
From: Max
Subject: Re: You're dead

What are you on about? You were the one asking for the password! I haven't been near it for months.

To: Ruth
From: O.B.
Subject: What's going on?

Izzy's just told me you're about to report me to the college for hacking into e-mails. It wasn't me. I sent one message for a joke and that's all, I swear. The stag thing has nothing to do with me. I'd hardly send out that myself, would I?
Sam O'Brien

To: Ruth
From: Izzy
Subject: O.B.

Hi Ruth
Much as I hate to say it, he's got a point. It may not be him. Report it to the college by all means, but I don't think it'd be fair to drop him in it.
(Attachment: What's going on?)

My pulse is going crazy. I've never felt so exhilarated.

To: Ben
From: Mandy
Subject: 'Monkey100'

I found this in my inbox today. Want to explain?
(Attachment: Ben sandwich)

To: Mandy
From: Ben
Subject: Re: 'Monkey 100'

Who sent you this? OK, I did some stupid stuff when I was on Finn's stag. I know it's no defence for acting like a complete dickhead, but it didn't mean anything and it was ages before we got together.

It's really immature, I know, but some of us had an encrypted file about the stuff that happened in Spain. That's where this is from. Any idea how it got to you?
Ben

To: Ben
From: Mandy
Subject: Re: 'Monkey 100'

Ben, I don't really care what you got up to. Just thought you should know, because there's someone breaking into people's e-mails and it could be the same person.
Mand
PS I think you should have an Aids test.

To: O.B., Max, Lewis, Finn, Tony, Luke
From: Ben
Subject: Stag

Is one of you sending stuff from the 'Keeper of the Stag' file to other people? If so, grow up, you're not funny. If not, any idea who's found out the password? Either way, delete the file.
Ben

To: Ben
From: Tony
Subject: Re: Stag

Oh yeah, my house is undergoing emergency renovations, my mum was nearly killed and has disappeared in a state of trauma – all this puts me *so* in the mood to play japes on my fellow stags.
Tony

To: Mandy
From: Ben
Subject: Re: 'Monkey 100'

Mand, I hope we're OK after that e-mail. I never pretended that I didn't have a past, but I'm really sorry you had to read about it like that. I've moved on a lot since then. I'll take the test if you want me to. Are we still OK for tonight?
Ben

To: Ben
From: Mandy
Subject: Re: 'Monkey 100'

I wasn't trying to get at you. It's just the thought of someone snooping around in my mail really freaks me out. Remember you received that e-mail that should've been for Cindy? For all we know, it could be the same person doing this. Will you e-mail all your contacts and find out if they know anything?
Mandy
PS Course we are.

To: Cindy
From: Ben
Subject: Hello

Hi Cind
How are things? Sorry it's been a while. Mandy's probably told you what happened at work. Still haven't got my head round it. I'm taking some time off, trying to chill out a bit. Just have to see how it goes when I'm back on duty. How's Holly?

I bet you're wondering what this e-mail's really about – well, here goes. Heard something today that worried me. Won't bore you with the details, but it seems like someone's been breaking into people's e-mail accounts. Mandy thinks it could be the same person that sent me one of her messages to you, can't remember when, months ago. Don't think I need to tell you why this rings alarm bells. Can you make sure you kill off all those old e-mails from the time just after you left? You've probably done this already. Anyway, it could be nothing, but just in case. Give my love to Holly.
Ben

I'm too excited to be frightened. This is fantastic – panic and chaos, with me at the centre of it all, invisible. Right now I'm fighting the urge to go to the window, throw it open and lean out into the night air. I'm the king of the world!!

20 June 2001   12:01am

Nothing new among Lewis's mail; maybe the state of play between Ruth and Finn is low down his list of priorities. I head for Ruth and find this little beauty…

To: All Students
From: Principal's Office
Subject: Violation of e-mail privacy

A number of students have reported suspected attempts to hack into their private e-mail accounts.

I wish to remind you that any such activity is in direct violation of the college's code of conduct governing students' rights to privacy. If it is happening on our premises, it is also a gross misuse of Hollyoaks Community College equipment.

Any student found to be gaining unauthorised access to e-mails will be subject to disciplinary measures, which may include permanent exclusion from college.

It is in all our interests to stop this happening. Any information will be handled in the strictest confidence.
Paul Davies
Principal

Wow, *I'm* scared. With the combined brainpower of HCC on my case, it can only be a matter of time before my goose is cooked. Yeah, right. A pathetic scare tactic, that's all this is.

> To: Finn
> From: Ruth
> Subject: Need your advice
>
> Couldn't tell you about this earlier, Deva was too busy. I had another misdirected e-mail last night, one of Geri's again, telling Anna how 'into' Lewis she is. You're probably thinking 'not again', but something about this really disturbs me. And I'm starting to wonder if Geri is doing all this deliberately as a way of telling me 'I'm with Lewis, deal with it.' I may be a paranoid bitch-from-hell, but you know how she's been encouraging students to complain to the college about this e-mail thief. Could it be a smoke screen to hide what she's doing? Maybe she somehow got hold of the e-mail where I moaned about her being insensitive for sleeping with Lewis, and this is her retaliation? Help!! I know I've probably gone off into the deep end here but be honest, is there any part of you that thinks I could be right? There's no one else I can talk to about this. Anyway, I'm not going to mention this latest one to her. I'll watch her and try to suss out if she's waiting for a reaction.
> Ruth

I feel like I've planted a huge suspicion bomb. Everyone's started to hear it ticking, but they're too busy panicking to work out what to do. Time to see how far the hysteria has spread.

> To: Adam
> From: Izzy
> Subject: E-mails

I hate to bore you with reality – I realise nothing's more important to you than your film. You may have heard about problems with e-mail security. I understand your brother was on the stag trip. Would you mind asking him if he's got any idea who's doing this?
Izzy

To: Izzy
From: Adam
Subject: Re: E-mails

Don't undersell yourself, Iz, you know I've always got time for you… Don't think I can help though. I'll ask Luke, but there's no way he's involved in this. Why don't we attempt a face-to-face next time?
Adam

To: Zara
From: Adam
Subject: (No subject)

Call me on my mobile as soon as you get this. URGENT.
Adam

To: Zara
From: Adam
Subject: (No subject)

I'm not messing, Zara. Are you in school? CALL ME.

To: Kim
From: Lisa
Subject: Hello

How are you? Got an e-mail from Naomi saying she 'thought' you and Jason were back together. Can you confirm or deny, please?! (Oops, shouldn't have slagged him off…)

Nothing much happening here. Except Dad found the condoms they gave us at school and went mental with me, accusing me of giving it up for every other boy in Chester. I think I'm getting to the point where nothing he can do can upset me any more, because I was thinking, can we get this over with please? My other thought: if only you knew. Like I've got boys beating each other up to go out with me. No boy has even looked my way since I came to Hollyoaks, but I'm the borderline-square, silent weirdo so what should I be – surprised? (*I* wouldn't go out with me, at least not the me I've been stuck with since I started here. Which *so* isn't the way I really am. Why have I done this to myself, Kim? It drives me mental.) Anyway, the only surprise was that Dan – shock, horror – actually stood up to Dad and told him to leave me alone.

At least I'm not the only one who's guilty until proven innocent. Zara's brother, Adam, is accusing her of breaking into e-mails from students at Dan's college, just because she sent this joke thing months ago, mmm, that's fair. She just e'd me to say he went ballistic, but she gave as good as she got. He still doesn't believe her though. Oh, well. Remember my theory about other people's crap times making me feel better? It still works.
Lisa

To: Ben
From: Adam
Subject: E-mail security

All right
Sorry to trouble you, mate, just a quick one about the 'stag file' getting broken into. You haven't let your darling god-daughter in on the password, have you? Because if you have, I think the mystery is over. I'd be grateful if we could keep it between us – no real harm's been done and I think I've given her a preventative scare.
Adam

To: Ben
From: Mandy
Subject: Re: Zara

Hi… Sorry I couldn't get in touch earlier, I'm really behind on the fashion show details. (I'll make it up to you tomorrow in the 'special way', deal?!?) I was thinking about what you said earlier. I don't think Zara knows enough to be able to get into so many people's accounts. I've been getting a really strange vibe off you-know-who, though. Especially since she helped me and Luke recover all those files we thought we'd lost. I was grateful and everything, but she was so smug, as if she was waiting for it to happen. Do you think she could be the hacker? It makes sense if you think about it. She's got enough computer knowledge. Luke could've given her the stag password and she could have got all the other people's passwords from watching them in college. You know the way she comes into a room and makes you jump because she never says anything until she's right up close to you. And she always knows so much about us. She'd have loved to see my face after reading that thing about you on the stag night.

Can't believe I'm saying this, she's supposed to be my friend. Can't get it out of my mind though. I hate this. What do you think? Mandy

To: Mandy
From: Ben
Subject: Re: Zara

you'll have 2 ask her, just come out with it, she can't mess you around like this. i can see it's doing your head in, don't want her reading our private stuff, saying who knows what to luke. i hate late shifts, want & need you bad, slow & all night. if u get this, reply straight away, margaret's on fag break, b quick.

To: Ben
From: Mandy
Subject: Re: Zara

I can't. I work with her, Luke lives with her, everything's tied up together – what if I'm wrong?

To: Mandy
From: Ben
Subject: Re: Zara

what if you're right? i think you're scared of her (don't go off on one.) whatever, i've got an idea. send me your address book. i won't target her or use your name, just want her to know everyone's serious. i've had it up to here with her.

He wrote this a few hours later:

To: Adam, Chloe, Taylor, Alex, Ruth, Geri, Izzy, Tony, Anna,
          Lewis, Finn, Luke, Laura, Max, O.B.
From: Ben
Subject: Fun's over

All right, we all know what's going on. It doesn't just affect students.
The college seems to think a few empty words are enough, but I
don't. We've got to show whoever's doing this that we're coming
after them. Send me dates, times and who to/who from of all e-
mails you shouldn't have received.
Ben Davies

Uh-oh, you've overstepped the mark, my friend. Wanting to catch
me is one thing, but doing something about it – sorry, can't let that
happen. He sent the e-mail just two hours ago, so there should be
time. I go into as many inboxes as I can and delete Ben's message.
That still leaves a handful of people whose passwords I haven't
cracked, but I've done all I can. Just one more precaution to take.

To: Ben
From: Monkey 100
Subject: Read this now

So you fancy yourself as a crusader for e-mail privacy? Well, I think
I know why.
    A 'borrowed' car. A girl left for dead in a dark, filthy ditch. An
innocent man hounded by police while you stood by and did
nothing. Am I painting any pictures here? All right, how about this:
your career in ruins. Your girlfriend abandoning you. Your dad
turning his back on you. You sharing a jail cell with three other
blokes.
    I know what you did to Anna Green. I know you were the
passenger, but you were every bit as guilty as the driver. Don't kid
yourself. You could've chosen to do the right thing. You didn't. All
you cared about was getting caught.
    I've got it all in black and white, your own words, ready to bang
off to all your friends and the most senior officer in Chester police –
someone who'll make sure Daddy won't be able to dig you out with
a few words in the right ears.

> You've hurt someone I care about. Now you're irritating me.
> Stop poking around in other people's business, or the nightmare
> scenario will unfold.

I don't like playing the hard man, but I've got no choice. If I let Ben's
bandwagon gain momentum, I'm the one who's going to get
crushed. Got to protect myself.

To: Izzy
From: Chloe
Subject: E-snooper

This is either going to sound really obvious or really vindictive,
depending on how well you know me. Been thinking about this
e-mail thing. I know everyone's getting ultra-suspicious, but there's
an obvious candidate for who's doing it. Anti-social computer nerd,
hmm, who could that be… That's all I want to say for now. I've got
no proof, but let's be honest – this fits his loveable personality like a
loveable-personality-shaped glove.
Chloe

To: Sis-sis
From: Izzy
Subject: Hi from your baby sis

Hi Bella
I've been *soooooo* restrained saving this when I've wanted to tell you
for days. Got an e-mail from Adam a few days ago. Anyway, it wasn't
meant for me but some ex of his called Kerri. (Something's going on
with the e-mails, seems like some weirdo is getting his or her kicks
by re-routing messages.) But oh my God, Bella, it was all about me,
how he wants me back and how he regrets messing things up. He
said he wanted to show I was right to have faith in him. I know he
was probably ratted when he wrote it but still… Reading it gave me
all sorts of weird tingly feelings. I haven't thought about anything else
for days. I've seen him a few times round college but I've avoided
him. We've even exchanged a few e-mails, but we've been totally
normal (i.e. grotty with each other). I want to say I deleted it, thought
'losers, weepers' and did a girl power salute, but I feel so strange

about it, Bella. Maybe I was too hard on him. When things were good, they were amazing, really, and there's no point kidding myself that they weren't. The thing I can't work out is why he was telling this to his ex, not to me. If I felt he was genuine, I might be willing to listen to whatever he's got to say... So what do I do? Wait for him to ask? How long – until he's lost interest? Need benefit of my big sis's wisdom.

Love and hugs

Iz

To: Izzy
From: O.B.
Subject: Hi

Hi Izzy

Got the e-mail from the principal's office. So what's going on with that now? Was my name mentioned? Just wondered in case you knew anything.

   Anyway, see you at rehearsals.

Sam O'Brien

To: O.B.
From: Izzy
Subject: Re: Hi

Unclench, Mr Understudy. I think everyone's realised we're dealing with someone way beyond your capabilities. If you're trying to gain popularity round college, you'd be better off reviving your rap career as the Notorious O.B.

Izzy

To: Alex
From: Izzy
Subject: Security

Any idea who the mystery hacker is? I just thought you might have noticed one of your computer friends getting nervous, since everyone's so angry.

   Spoke to the IT department this afternoon. They think they'll have worked out who's doing it in the next day or so.

Izzy

Nice attempted bluff, Izzy. 'Next day or so'. As if! OK, one final trawl through the main players' mail before I go to bed.

I find this. It was sent ten minutes ago:

To: Dennis Richardson, c/o HMP Blackwood
From: Lewis
Subject: (No subject)

Hope you get a kick out of this, you bastard. Yeah, you're gonna love hearing what your son has done this time. Had two thousand pounds and put it all on the wheel, and I doubled it – four grand in front of me. Could've walked away, but I put it on again and blew the lot. That's the addiction, yes it's true what everyone says, I'm an ADDICT and I got this sickness from you, alcohol or gambling, same disease. Thanks, Dad, you made me hit the girl I loved more than my life, and now you're making me piss away everything I've got left. Remember Kurt Benson? You used to teach him. Well, Ruth loved him and he's dead, and I pretended to be him to feed the sickness you put in me. I lost it all so I found more, because I have to survive and I'll show you I won't always be like this, I'm so much better than you, Dad. You know what I hate most of all, you've made me a liar, just like you. You lied to Mum and Mandy and said sorry and it'll never happen again, and you lied to me and pretended you were a good dad. You lied so I didn't know what you were doing and I couldn't stop you. And now I'm lying because I'm desperate, and what else can I do? I can't keep this up and there are people who want me dead. You'd love that, but it's not going to happen, I'm going to turn everything around. Yeah, everything. You're the one who'll die miserable and hating yourself.

The top of my skull turns icy, the way it did when all this started. Got to calm down. The blood's thumping in my ears like I've run a marathon. So that's what he did to Ruth. I just can't believe it. I try, but I can't imagine it. Lewis, an abuser. How could he be, after living through it with his mum and dad?

I can't keep this quiet. But how do I go public? And if I did, would anyone believe me? I've got no evidence. And if it ever came out that

I was a hacker, my credibility would vanish. Yet I can't do nothing. So – what?

I sit for an hour, trying to work it out. My best move – my only move – is to let him think no one's watching him and hope he lets slip something he can't wriggle out of, once he's confronted with it. Then I try to decipher the stuff about Kurt Benson. My only guess is that he used Kurt's ID to borrow money which he then gambled away. Maybe that's how he got the money he offered to Finn to buy the club. Who knows?

There's only one clear thought in my mind, rising above all the questions: Geri. She needs to know about this. I have to tell her, it's my responsibility – just not now, not while half of Chester wants my head on a stake. Another thought that won't go away: if not now, then when? I'll sleep on it.

22 June 2001   11:05pm

Couldn't sleep last night. All I've eaten today is a bag of crisps and a chocolate bar, but I don't feel hungry. I'm running on 100% pure nervous energy. I've got a major dilemma – or it's got me, more like. To send or not to send Lewis's mail to Geri? I try to weigh it up. What if I do nothing? Lewis could do to Geri what he did to Ruth – maybe worse, considering the state he's in. If I send it, she'd at least have a warning that he's not all he seems. But she might not believe it was real, and then she'd have a big, shiny reason to step up her campaign against the mail thief. Things are dangerous enough for me as it is. And who's to say that splitting them up is a good thing? For all I know, being with Geri could be what Lewis needs to put his life back together. Trouble is, I'm hearing another little voice inside my head: *She deserves to know what she's getting into.*

I can't handle this. If I send Geri this e-mail, I'm over. The only reason why they haven't found me is that they haven't looked hard enough. The second this hits Geri's inbox, all that will change. But there's something else stopping me too. I've read Lewis's e-mail again and although I don't want to pity him – what he did was worse than terrible, nothing can excuse him hitting Ruth – I can't help it. I pity him more than I want to see him punished.

But still… Geri. I'll think about it.

To: Finn
From: Ruth
Subject: Geri

I'm so confused!! She's acting totally normal, but is it real normal or fake normal? Crapping hell. I'm *so* sure she sent it. Totally worked myself up now. Maybe I should say something.

To: Ruth
From: Finn
Subject: Re: Geri

Maybe you should say something, yes./No, best not to say anything.*
(*delete according to whatever you've already decided.)
PS Nothing from Vic. When do I officially give up hope? Probably should have done already – just can't.

To: Geri
From: Ruth
Subject: More e-mail problems

Hi… Just in case I don't see you today, I've had another one of your e-mails sent to me (meant for Anna). Thought I should warn you. Wish the college would get its act together. See you later.
Ruth

To: Anna
From: Geri
Subject: It's happened again

I'm so angry I want to throw up. Ruth just told me she got another one of my e-mails to you. That piece of scum is at it again. Too embarrassed to ask Ruth, but please don't let it be that one about Lewis. I've really had enough. What does it take to get college admin off their backsides? Snotty e-mail on its way. One other

thing, Anna. I heard Chloe and Izzy saying they thought it might be Alex. Have to say it wouldn't surprise me. Any thoughts?
Geri

To: Admin Dept
From: Geri
Subject: E-mail security

My private e-mail has been broken into yet again. I appreciate that the college is aware of this problem, but can you give us some idea when it's going to be sorted out? You're probably also aware that many of the students believe they're being fobbed off with empty words. Perhaps you can let us know what you're doing to catch the culprit. Anyone with access to personal information is an obvious threat to student safety. I don't think it's unreasonable to expect a secure environment considering what you take from us in fees.
Geri Hudson

To: Geri
From: Anna
Subject: Re: It's happened again

I don't know. Maybe.

I looked for you this afternoon – I really need to talk. Alex has had a second test. He is fertile. He said he went for it after you spoke to him about his responsibilities (thanks). Then came the apology, only he didn't quite get the response he expected. I totally blew up at him. Then he said he loved me and was sorry for everything he said about me being unfaithful, and we sort of decided to get back together. I've made it sound like everything's settled but it so isn't. He wants me to have an abortion. He just assumed it was what I'd want too, like he was doing me a favour for suggesting it. Don't know why I'm surprised, but it hurts because I thought (only for a few seconds, but still) that he was offering to support me whatever decision I made. I couldn't have been more wrong. He wants to 'take care' of me, but what he really means is get rid of the problem, i.e. if I want him, the baby has to go. I knew it was an option but I never thought about it properly. Now I'm more confused than ever. I've always hated the idea of aborting a child, but I feel like whatever I decide, I won't be doing it for myself, I'll be doing it to either get at Alex or keep him happy. I'm so confused. At lunchtime, I was single and together. Now I'm half a couple and all over the place. Work that one out. I've tried and I can't. Can I come round later?

Anna

To: Ben
From: Mandy
Subject: Any response?

Did anyone reply to your e-mail? Get an answer from Laura?

Mandy

PS Wear those silky boxers when u come round tomorrow. (Don't say they're not clean, because they won't be on long enough for me to mind. XXX)

To: Mandy
From: Ben
Subject: Re: Any response?

Steady!! Yeah, she said she'd been sent something of Tony's once. Sounded pretty genuine, I don't think it's her. So can we concentrate on the interesting stuff from now on? (Tell me more... Gave Margaret a blueberry thing so I've got extra time... You'll be amazed how many fantasies I can cram into five minutes.)

At least he's been taken care of. Geri's more worrying. I can't pass anything onto her while she's so determined to uncover me. It'd be suicidal. Hold on, this just arrived in Mandy's inbox:

To: Mandy, Geri, Izzy, Ruth, Taylor, Chloe, Adam, Finn, Lewis, Tony, Anna, O.B., Max
From: Alex
Subject: Snoop-proof your e-mails

Amigos, amigos, get a grip. Anyone would think you've never had a crazed hacker on your case before. Let Uncle Alex restore some good karma round here. There's a simple way to stop these shenanigans. Contact me, and I will provide a program and some easy-to-follow instructions. Hey presto, your privacy will be intact once more.

Only ten quid, and as I'm Mr Trust, you can give it to me when you sée me. Watch this space for news of your friendly, neighbourhood cybersnoop's ID – I'm on the trail.

Alex

Uh-oh.

Time to focus. *Hard*. How serious is this? Only one honest answer: very. He could be bluffing, but then again, why would he? He's the only geek I know who's obsessive enough to follow through on his threat. I'm pretty sure he means what he says about the program – whether it works or not is another matter. As for promising to unmask me, I think it's just a crowd-pleaser to win him some popularity. Can't help feeling a bit cheated that he's making money out of my efforts.

What should I do? Whatever it is, it has to be fast – as in five minutes ago. I need to gather as much dirt on Alex as I can. No point trying his account, it'll be safeguarded. Anna's the obvious target. I slam in passwords – can't hit the keys fast enough.

annagreen	Please re-enter password
samsmallwood	Please re-enter password
alexbell	Please re-enter password

I'm panting, not breathing. Got to calm down. But my stomach feels like an angry animal is trapped inside, trying to chew its way out. What if Anna's already installed Alex's program and it works? Can't let this thought stop me trying. OK, she studies architecture. *Think*.

architecture	Please re-enter password
building	Please re-enter password
drawingboard	Please re-enter password

I try the names of all the architects I've heard of, rack my brains for her mum and dad's names. Nothing. I've been at this over an hour. What if this is Alex's program at work? I have to carry on. My fingers are still moving, but my brain's pretty much shut down.

keepout	Please re-enter password
fortress	Please re-enter password
impenetrable	Please re-enter password
uncrackable	Please re-enter password
private	Password accepted

No *way*.

At least there's someone up there who's not out to destroy me. There are so many e-mails here. I've got to find what matters and fast. First this, from months ago:

To:	Anna
From:	Sam
Subject:	Alex

I know I'm the last person you want to hear from, but I hope you'll read this. Nothing I say can make up for the way I ran out on you. I won't try because I don't want you to get angry and not read the rest of this. I'm worried about Alex. I got an e-mail from him today, timed 3:36am. I get the feeling he's told you about this infertility thing, so I don't think I'm breaking his confidence. He sounded in a really bad way (completely bladdered as well). He said his life was a 'dead end' and that he couldn't see any future for himself. You know what I'm thinking. He's a loner, never talks about stuff, and I think he could try and do something stupid. If anyone can get through to him, it's you. Anyway, I replied to him, tried to do the best I could.

Don't know if you're interested, but Nikki and I have been history for months. We backpacked round Europe after we left Chester, and got jobs at this bar near Cannes. Worked out fine until I happened to see Nikki, supposedly on a late shift, doing it with the bar manager on the bonnet of his jeep. As far as I know (or care) she's still there (France, not the bonnet). It's not like I'm in a position to judge. Now I'm back at home. I'm working three days a week in the local offy and trying to decide what next. Loads of rows with Mum, I've got a long way to go before I prove I'm not just a waste of food and oxygen. Sorry about all the damage I did to you but I know you're a strong enough person to get over it, stronger than I'll ever be. I suppose what I mean is that I'm a coward and you're not. Take care of Alex.

Sam

To: Alex
From: Anna
Subject: (No subject)

Next time just say you don't want to talk, instead of blanking me in front of the whole media lab. I'm sorry I interfered, OK? You can say we're over, fine, but don't pretend I don't exist when all I'm guilty of is trying to help. My dad was unfaithful and yours is gay, but they both lied and we're both having to deal with it. I avoided my dad for months but it really hurt me, he was on my mind all the time. When I spoke to him again, I stopped being obsessed. I don't want to see you going through the same thing because, if you're anything like me, you'll just regret the time you wasted. I don't expect you to agree with me, I just want a bit of respect.

Anna

News to me. This sounds useful too:

To: Anna
From: Alex
Subject: You

Been thinking about what you told me (good move sneaking out before I woke up this morning, by the way). Want your stuff off the barge. Go and stay with Adam Morgan. You've obviously been dying to make it official ever since you did it unprotected. Tell him your bit of news while you're there.

To: Alex
From: Anna
Subject: Re: You

This is the last time I'll say this: you're the father of this baby, not Adam, unless I can get pregnant from a conversation. I bet you haven't even had the guts to ask him.

To: Alex
From: Anna
Subject: Re: You

Fine, I'm out of there. I'll get my stuff later.

I send Alex's 'You' e-mail to Izzy – one scare's not going to stop me having a bit of fun. Time to get busy.

To: Alex
From: Monkey 100
Subject: Dad

Been busy, haven't we? Just a word of warning. Make my identity your business and no one will be able to hear your name without the words 'gay dad' springing to mind. Personally, I don't see what all the fuss is about, but we're talking about you, not me.
Cheers

It's a dirty trick and I know I won't sleep soundly tonight. I never wanted to go on the attack. But here I am, doing what all rats do when they're cornered.

23 June 2001   2:55am

Funny how I used to *enjoy* sitting here. I've been putting it off for hours, psyching myself up to check my e-mail. Nothing from Alex. It's too early to assume I've silenced him, but hopefully I've shaken him up a bit. I go for Lewis's e-mail.

access denied

Uh-oh. Try Finn's.

access denied

Damn. Alex's program must have worked. I try Geri.

access denied

They're all blocked: Izzy, Anna, Adam. Lucky I kept copies of all Lewis's most incriminating mail. I try Max. No entry. Lisa. *At last.* I can get into Steph's, too – no one's thought to send them the program.

> To: Steph
> From: Abby
> Subject: Your lost cherry
>
> Has he called/texted you? He's supposed to be coming round again,
> isn't he? E me if you've done it again!! You still haven't said how it
> feels to be a non-virgin…
> Ab

> To: Abby
> From: Steph
> Subject: Re: Your lost cherry
>
> Just texted, he's on his way. Shall I set up a webcam for you?! You
> can wait till tomorrow!! I don't know, I just feel sort of different.
> Steph

> To: Steph
> From: Abby
> Subject: Re: Your lost cherry
>
> Different how? Oh God, remember that video they showed us in
> Year 8 with that spoddy girl who'd just done it going, 'I feel like a
> real woman' – is that you, Steph??
> Ab

To: Abby
From: Steph
Subject: Re: Your lost cherry

OK, I feel less like a little girl, will that do you? Now go away, I've got to sort my hair.
Steph

To: Lisa
From: Zara
Subject: Hi

Writing this cos I can't sleep. Just been yelling at Adam – he's still asking me if I'm 'sure' I'm not breaking into people's e-mails. No, I'm not sure, Adam, maybe I did it by accident when I was trying to download celebrity genitals!?!

The other thing that's bugging me is Steph thinking she's it. I couldn't believe her coming out with that 'I've lost my virginity – Abby's next' stuff. I'm not being a bitch, but (a) Abby's not all that, (b) she hasn't even got a proper boyfriend and (c) it could be you for all she knows. She's so up herself sometimes. As if her 'relationship' means more than me and Brian, just because they've had sex. I feel sorry for her really, she's being used and she doesn't even know it.
Za

To: Kim
From: Lisa
Subject: Hi

Unsubtle question alert: do you reckon you and Jason will do it soon? I'm only asking cos it's what Zara and that lot have been talking about today, and now I can't stop thinking about it. It just seems so far away, even having a boyfriend. Can you imagine Dad? Boyfriend = sex = staying out = not knowing where I am = forget it. I've tried to stop myself thinking about boys cos I know how much hassle I'm going to get. There are three lads I really like, but even if I did something about it, I'd probably mess it up cos I'd be so nervous. If I get a boyfriend, it's going to stir up so many memories of everything, and all the arguments that went on just before it happened and our family got torn apart. (Don't need to tell you this, you heard enough of them.) It's so easy for Dan and Lee, they can do what they want. I can't keep letting Dad think I'm this little child who never thinks about sex, but if I do something about it, there's going to be such a massive fight and my family have been through enough. I'm scared that if I keep pretending for too long, the person I really am will just shrivel up and die. Say something reassuring, Kim, even if it's crap, I don't care. I just want to stop feeling like I'm the last person alive.

Lisa

When am I going to find out what the 'it' is that happened in Lisa's past? Got to be honest with myself – maybe never, if Alex's program spreads. I try Ben and Mandy – no access. O.B. Hey, I'm *in*. Trust him to be too lazy to install it.

To: O.B.
From: Chloe
Subject: Need 2 talk

You in for lectures this pm? I need a word.

To: Chloe
From: O.B.
Subject: Re: Need 2 talk

Giving them a miss, got to get essay in by the morning. What's up?

To: O.B.
From: Chloe
Subject: Re: Need 2 talk

I got a weird vibe off Alex just now. I asked him if he was getting any closer to working out who's snooping on the e-mails. He looked really awkward and said yeah, but that he couldn't say anything about it right now. It started me thinking, especially about my tenner and all the others he's raking in. Any thoughts?
Chloe

To: Chloe
From: O.B.
Subject: Re: Need 2 talk

Haven't installed mine yet. You saying you think it's him?

To: O.B.
From: Chloe
Subject: Re: Need 2 talk

I don't know. But if I were you, I'd bin it. I've just taken mine off. I've
got a bad feeling about it. Whether it was him or not, what if his
program makes it dead easy for him to read our mail?

To: Chloe
From: O.B.
Subject: Re: Need 2 talk

Captain Paranoia! I always thought it might be Theo, myself.

To: O.B.
From: Chloe
Subject: Re: Need 2 talk

No way, it's not his style. Why don't you send Alex an e-mail, ask
him same as me, see what he says, then let us know.

To: Chloe
From: O.B.
Subject: Re: Need 2 talk

OK, I'll try it. Sorry to insult gadget-boy... always knew you had a
festering thing for him.

To: O.B.
From: Chloe
Subject: Re: Need 2 talk

As if! Where'd you get that from?

To: Alex
From: O.B.
Subject: Who is it?

Alright
You cracked it then? Some cynical people are saying the whole
thing's a money-spinning scam but I said, Alex? Surely not. So
come on, mate, who is it?
Sam O'Brien

To: O.B.
From: Alex
Subject: Re: Who is it?

If I wanted to make money, I wouldn't have spent days writing a
program just for a lousy couple of hundred quid. I have worked out
who's been doing it, but I can't tell you yet because I want to catch
them at it. How come you haven't installed your program? Until you
put it on, you might as well be sending all your mail straight to the
hacker's inbox.
Alex

To: Chloe
From: O.B.
Subject: Alex

Here it is. What do you reckon?
(Attachment: Re. Who is it?)

To: O.B.
From: Chloe
Subject: Re: Alex

It *so* is him! 'Can't tell us', well duh, I wonder why! Come *on*, if you
found out who was doing it, could you really stop yourself telling
the whole world? It's the perfect scam – start a scare, then sit back
and rake it in. We've all been so off our heads with panic we've
forgotten what a slimy piece of work he really is. This is the man
who hid a python in his bedroom, don't forget. (Yes I'm well aware
what your filthy mind is making of this, and I'm choosing to ignore

it.) There's no way we can let this happen. He's caused enough misery round here. I'm putting out a warning.
Chloe

To: Matt, Mandy, Izzy, Anna, Geri, Tony, Ruth, O.B., Max, Alex
From: Chloe
Subject: Warning

I'm pretty sure we've all been victims of a scam by Alex. He claims he's found the mystery hacker but 'can't reveal his name'. I, for one, think it's all been a scheme to separate us from our hard-earned cash. And for all we know, he's using the program to get easy access to our mail, so I advise you to get rid of it ASAP. Alex, if I'm wrong, prove it. (Pass this on to anyone else who's used the program.)
Chloe Bruce

Thank you. Chloe, I want to hug you. You might just have saved my life. You wouldn't think it if you saw me, though. My sweat has turned cold and I'm shivering. I'm seeing little black dots swimming around somewhere between my eyes and the screen. I should send Lewis's mail to Geri right now. I just *can't*. I've pushed my luck to breaking point. Now I've got the chance to walk away unharmed. Sending things to Geri would be like throwing away a lifebelt and choosing to drown. *What about Geri, though*? Whatever. Can't think straight.

24 June 2001   1:20pm

Couldn't wait until tonight. Got to make this quick. Excellent, Geri's junked the program. So have Izzy, Ben and Mandy.

To: Alex
From: Geri
Subject: You rat

It's true, isn't it? Well done, you've outdone yourself this time. The only surprise in all this is that you kept us wondering for so long. Otherwise, it's totally in character – just ask Anna. Do it again and I'll report you for harassment.

To: Alex
From: Izzy
Subject: (No subject)

This is so like you. You are a sad, sad little man.

To: Alex
From: Ben
Subject: Dickhead

Do you know how pathetic you are? Go anywhere near mine or Mandy's mail and you're going to need physio before you use a keyboard again.
Ben

To: Geri, Izzy
From: Alex
Subject: Re: You rat

You should know better than to trust Chloe's opinion of me. She's suffering from a fatal combination of serious prejudice and mornings spent in front of *Scooby Doo*. Watch my lips – I am not the hacker. I've got a life, thanks. As for knowing who it is, I worked it out more or less straight away. Without catching him at it, it's my word against his. Just think about that before you make me the target of your witch hunt, OK kids?
Alex
PS Ben – you've lost me, mate. Is this post-traumatic stress talking, or what?

Nice try, Alex. He can talk the talk, but no one's going to believe it. He sounds like what he is – a man who's scared.

My server just flashed the 'You Have Mail' icon.

To: Monkey 100
From: Alex
Subject: Read this carefully

I know who you are. Feel free to tell the world about my dad. Who's
got more to lose, me or you? I don't think you'll have any trouble
working that one out. The only way you'll keep me silent is to cough
up £3,000. If you don't, I'll spread your name and picture across the
Net. I'll turn you into a piece of junk mail that'll turn up in every
office, home and college from Chester to Peru. You've met your
match and then some. So what now? The ball's in your court.
Alex

I almost make it to the waste-paper bin before throwing up.

24 June 2001   12:30am

Think. *Really* think. My brain got me into this, it can get me out. But
all I've got in my head is a little diagram: every bit of trouble I've
ever been in = The Loft; this = Wembley Stadium. I keep trying to
chill, or focus, or do whatever will make my stomach lie down and
shut up.

I've got to prepare myself for the worst. At least everyone's
ditched Alex's program. I've got to trawl through the mail and try to
arm myself with whatever secrets I can. So if Alex reveals my
identity, I can flood everyone's inboxes with gossip and, hopefully,
who I am will seem trivial by comparison. *If.* Wishful thinking. It's
definitely a case of *when*.

To: Carol
From: Tony
Subject: My dream

Hello baby
I day-dreamed about you when I was in town today, and before I
knew it I'd bought a set of black silk sheets for the bed. When the
time comes, when the miles no longer separate us, I'll carry you up

the stairs, tear off your clothes and you'll feel my cool sheets against your milky skin. Then it'll be Barcelona every day and we'll make love like there's no tomorrow, except Sunday when we'll chill and I'll cook you my special roast. Go out on deck tonight and look up at the sky. Never forget that the same moon shines on us both, sweet lady. Choose a star and maybe my dream will come true sooner than I dare hope.

Yours always
Tony

To: Tony
From: Carol
Subject: Re: My dream

Dear Tony

Thanks for making my day and a silver wedding couple from Derby very happy (is happy the same as helpless with giggles?) Just two things. Only people over forty 'make love'. And you are, in fact, a very down-to-earth student landlord and chef, not the love child of Jamie Oliver and Craig David. But I am touched. I hate you now, you've only gone and made me homesick again. It will happen, I promise. Soon.

Carol

To: Finn
From: Tony
Subject: You bastard

In case that punch knocked it out of you, just making sure you get the message. I will never, EVER forgive you for what you've done to Mum. I will never EVER forgive you for lying to me, for feeding off my sympathy when I should've been putting your lights out. You're everything I always suspected and worse. Do yourself and everyone else a favour, pack your bags and go as far away from Chester as you can fly on last night's takings. You disgust me. If you had any decency, you'd disgust yourself. If you stick around, I'll do everything I can to make your life a living hell. Watch this space.

To: Carol
From: Finn
Subject: You were right

Can't remember when it was (except it was during a row), but you
said something which has stayed with me. You said some people
are meant to be in relationships and some are meant to be alone.
You said I was one of the latter. Well, you were right. Today's the day
everything crashed down on me. Victoria's officially gone for good.
There's no going back. She's cleared out her stuff. I've never felt
such a totally worthless failure in my life. I loved her, Carol. To set
the record straight from Barcelona, I loved you too. Since when has
that ever stopped me screwing up? No wonder she was sick of me.
I'm sick of me. Don't know why you or Vic got involved with me
anyway. All I want to do is move forward in my life and be someone
else, responsible, capable of being loved, someone I can respect.
But I've tried growing up, I've given it everything and it just won't
happen. What's wrong with me?

To: Finn
From: Carol
Subject: Re: You were right

We are in a bad way, aren't we? Finn, I've known some hopeless
cases in my time. You haven't quite made it into that league yet. Put
some music on, get lashed, do whatever it takes to get happy, OK?
And when you've got over your hangover, ask yourself this: what
did you get from that one-night stand that you didn't get from
Victoria? Cos these things happen for a reason. And if no one else
will say it, I will – she may have been a lovely woman, but she was
too old. There's growing up and there's booking a place in the
retirement home. Maybe next time you'll get it right.
Chin up mister
Carol

To: Finn
From: Ruth
Subject: Hi

Sorry to hear what happened with Tony. I've had bigger surprises though. I know I always say this, but I'm always around to talk if it'd help. It's not the time to go on about this, but I can't work John out at all. We keep doing this one step forwards, two steps back kind of thing, which makes me think I'm coming on too strong or something. So much has happened with Lewis and everything that I don't trust my instincts any more. I thought being with someone I had a lot in common with would make things simpler. But now I'm wondering if I'm mistaking friendship for something else...
Anyway, like you need to hear this now. Call me.
Ruth

To: Geri
From: Izzy
Subject: Two thousand pounds

How can anyone 'lose' £2,000? My team's searched the whole college and there's no sign of it. Come on, you must have an idea where you left it. There are so many people who worked hard for this, and they all trusted you. I'm not angry, I'm just really disappointed.
Izzy

To: Sis-sis
From: Izzy
Subject: Him

Bella, your sister is a free woman. I don't like saying things like this in case it's tempting fate, but I think I'm finally free of Adam. The bizarre thing is that it's thanks to that freak who's been hacking into e-mails and misdirecting things. I got this e-mail from Alex to Anna, accusing her of sleeping with Adam. Alex is a loon, so no idea whether it's true or not, but Anna *is* pregnant and Adam *is* (potentially at least) a slelparound hound, so who knows. I spent an entire morning wondering true or false while I was shopping for shoes, then when I was at the sandwich bar I had this flash and I suddenly realised it didn't matter. The only thing that *does* matter is, I don't trust him, and that rules out everything. God, he's coming over.
Love and hugs
Iz

To: Kerri
From: Adam
Subject: Your advice

Alright babe

How's San Francisco? Took your advice re. 'Number Two' (can we call her something else? You know what that means over here). Had a nice, mellow chat about nothing much, just passed the time, and I think I'm making progress. I hope so, because seeing her still does things to me I can't describe (not even to a tough-as-boots Aussie who used to do those things to me herself not so long ago). Have one for me.

Ad

To: Mandy
From: Ben
Subject: (No subject)

Sorry. This keeps happening and I always tell myself it's the last time. It's me. Sometimes it's been easier to start a row than talk about stuff since the fire and I'm so sorry, Mand. I should have been a lot stronger. I never thought I'd still be scared so long afterwards. It's changed the way I see everything, my life especially. It feels weird to know I'm not as strong as I thought I was. The thing is, I'm not just talking about the job. It's shaken my belief in everything, even us. It never really bothered me before, but I keep thinking about how we got together, all the sneaking around, deceiving Luke. I feel ashamed about all the rows about stupid things, all the suspicions. I'm worried cos it feels like we started out on really shaky ground, but you're so important to me now, I can't stand the thought of losing you. I couldn't have come through this without you. Just wanted you to know.

Ben

To: Dennis Richardson, c/o HMP Blackwood
From: Lewis
Subject: (No subject)

Yes it's that time again and I've had a skinful, bet you wish you were me. Bet you dream about opening the bottle, getting a glass, pouring it out, then drinking, yeah, it feels good, Dad, pity they don't have bars where you are. Cos if they did, you would do me a massive favour and drink yourself under the table and under the ground, and that's the only time when I'm going to be free of you, Dad. I want you to die, you understand? You sent Mandy a letter and she said you were depressed and this is good news, very good news, maybe you'll get so depressed I'll hear even better news one day soon.

To: Lewis
From: Dennis Richardson, c/o HMP Blackwood
Subject: Re: (No subject)

Lewis, internet access isn't that free and easy here, so if you're going to make the effort, at least try to be sober. I'm getting tired of receiving these rants whenever things are going wrong (which, it seems, is a gross understatement) in your life. I'm paying for my sins, mistakes, whatever you want to call them. I won't be held responsible for yours as well. You are an adult and you have free will, self-control. You choose your actions, not me. That's fact, no matter how much you wish it were otherwise. You're to blame for whatever you do, not me. You can change yourself, and I hope you do. But you can't change this: I held you in my arms when you were a baby, and I felt nothing but love for you, and hoped that you'd grow up to be a happy, fulfilled, loving and well-balanced man. Please read that e-mail you sent to me. Can you honestly say you're proud to have written it? Well, that's up to you, like everything else. It comes down to you and your conscience, just as it does for me. In the end, we're both alone.
Your father

To: Anna
From: Geri
Subject: Disaster

This can't be happening to me. Money can't just disappear. This is a nightmare. I was so together and careful. Everyone hates me, don't they? I've just had Izzy doing her schoolmistress bit. Not that I blame her this time. You've got to be some kind of idiot to mislay two grand. What am I going to do? There's nowhere else to look. It won't take long for people to start suspecting me. I know you've got problems of your own, but if you've got any advice…

Don't know what I'd have done without Lewis, he's being so sweet. I know I haven't known him long, but he's my rock, my anchor (you get the picture), the thing that stops me losing it completely and drifting around in a useless panic. He's so mature and stable (at last, a boyfriend I deserve for once in my life).
Geri

No prizes for guessing where Lewis got the wad of cash he blew on the roulette wheel.

Right now, I've got more pressing worries. I crash out addresses, re-routing e-mails at random. Doesn't matter who gets them. I go through my deleted items, duplicate and send out every bit of junk and chain mail I can find, weight-loss ads, easy loans, investment advice, get-rich-quick schemes – anything to add to the tidal wave. It's still missing something. *Think*.

Got it. I need to throw in some information that's so obviously untrue, people won't believe the revelation about me, either. Shouldn't take long…

To: Alex, Anna, Chloe, Geri, Izzy, Tony, Lewis, Finn, Max, O.B.,
         Ben, Mandy
From: Matt
Subject: Izzy Cornwell has two belly buttons

To: Alex, Geri, Izzy, Chloe, Tony, Lewis, Finn, Max, O.B., Ben,
         Matt, Mandy
From: Anna
Subject: Mrs Morgan was born a man

To: Alex, Anna, Geri, Izzy, Chloe, Tony, Lewis, Finn, Max, O.B.,
         Ben, Matt
From: Mandy
Subject: Tony has secret twins

To: Alex, Anna, Geri, Chloe, Tony, Lewis, Finn, Max, O.B., Ben
From: Izzy
Subject: Rat droppings found in Deva flapjacks

To: Alex, Izzy, Geri, Chloe, Tony, Lewis, Finn, Max, O.B., Ben
From: Anna
Subject: Theo is seeing two married women

Despite the dire situation I'm in, I almost start enjoying myself. But it's just escapism, a way of not thinking about what I *can't help* thinking about: Geri. If I'm going to send her Lewis's mail, I should do it now. But I know that it'll raise more questions – more dangers – than everything else I've done. No matter how I try to reason with myself, it ends up as one very simple, very difficult choice: Geri's Safety vs. My Survival.

24 June 2001   3:45am

Can't sleep. Have to do this. Time to stand up for what I believe in. I dig out Lewis's latest e-mail to his dad. I'm shaking as I send it to Geri.

25 June 2001   10:15am

Can't believe this started out as fun. Sending that e-mail to Geri may have eased my conscience for a few hours, but now I'm terrified by the thought of what I've done. I've sneaked home to use the computer but I'm too terrified to go to her inbox. I try Finn first.

sign-in failure

Hey? I try Lewis. Same message. I keep trying. Same for everyone else. Dead end. It takes me a couple of seconds to realise what's happened. What I did last night has had more drastic effects than I imagined. Everyone's shut down their accounts. Signed up for new ones, no doubt, with new addresses and new passwords.

I can't accept it at first. I feel like someone close to me has died. I haven't got the heart to start again. These last few months have wrecked my body and my mind. I never realised that a double life would mean double the fear. I should be thankful I'm escaping with my reputation intact. But have I done enough to warn people about Lewis? Well, if Geri's as close to him as she thinks she is, she'll find out the truth about him for herself soon enough.

Maybe I should have told her face to face. Except I couldn't. If that was the way things worked, I wouldn't have been intrigued enough to start this in the first place. Nothing that matters happens face to face, not any more.

It's been an incredible ride, but I'll never do this again. *Ever*. Just want to check my own e-mails and return to normal life.

To: Monkey 100
From: Alex
Subject: You

Bet you're thrilled, thinking you've won. Well, enjoy it while it lasts. You've labelled me a villain and I've done what hackers do – I've done some digging. And you won't believe who and what I've discovered. Well, you'll find out soon enough. You're right in thinking I don't get on with my dad, but I'm not homophobic, and neither is anyone else that I care about. Tell the world, I don't mind. If you think you can use prejudice to turn everyone against me, you're living on another planet. Must be a pretty freaky one if you think you've got the right to judge other people.
Alex

Getting butterflies in my stomach. Major butterflies. More like vultures getting excited around a fresh carcass. What *is* this?

To: Monkey 100
From: Tony
Subject: You

Don't bother to defend yourself. What you've done is despicable.
Who are you to go raking through people's lives and passing on
details as if you've got the moral high ground? Have you
conveniently forgotten the time you conned me out of my video
shop lease? Or when you maliciously drove up the price of
student accommodation by trying to outbid me when I bought my
houses? The thing that I find hardest to believe is that I used to
respect you.
Tony

To: Monkey 100
From: O.B.
Subject: Who's a naughty boy then?

Blimey, what are you like? Thanks to you, I could've got booted out
of college. You want to watch it, it's not like there aren't any
embarrassing stories knocking around about you. What about
getting into bed with your ex-wife on the day you married Helen?
Hash cakes at a rock festival in Wales also spring to mind. Think
you might have had something stronger, too, cos Max told me you
were lying in the spare room telling everyone to 'smell the sound of
purple' until he put a wet towel round your head.
O.B.
PS Won't say anything as long as we're quits on the money you lent
us for the CD.

To: Monkey 100
From: Anna
Subject: Why?

I thought we were friends. Why did you do this? So what if I'm
pregnant and Alex is the father? Are you so out of touch that you
think it's a big deal I'm not married? For the record, Cindy once
told me her sister Dawn was born before you and her mum got
round to tying the knot, so what point are you trying to make
exactly? Do you know how much distress you've caused?
Anna

To: Monkey 100
From: Helen
Subject: (No subject)

No wonder you decided not to go into work today. Is it true what everyone's saying? Why aren't you answering the phone? Is this what your 'insomnia' and your 'mountain of paperwork' have been about? You better have a damn good explanation if you're planning to set foot in the house tonight.
Helen

To: Monkey 100
From: Geri
Subject: You disgust me

Everyone's out for your blood, so I won't waste my time. All I want to say is this: Lewis is worth a million of you. Fake e-mails full of malicious lies will never change that. (What is wrong with you? I really think you need help, fast.)
Geri

To: Monkey 100
From: Angela Cunningham
Subject: How could you?

Someone called Alex Bell contacted me this morning. Well, since it was about you, I knew it couldn't have been *good* news. I know you'd like to forget about me, along with the rest of your past. What you've been up to may have come as a shock to everyone else, but to me it was a sickening reminder of something I've been trying to forget for years. I bet you haven't even told Helen about your days as a postman, have you? How about the day the police came to search the house for missing mail while Max was blowing out the candles on his second birthday cake? Now it seems you're intent on putting poor Tom through the same ordeal. Thanks for reminding me why our divorce was the happiest day of my life.
Angela

Game over.

I go to the window like I'm sleepwalking. For once there's no darkness to reflect my face, just my neighbour mowing the lawn and some kids passing by. I want my old life back so badly I can feel tears forming in my chest. I won't try to defend myself because there'd be no point. But despite what everyone thinks, the last thing I wanted was to judge anyone. I wanted some fun, a few thrills. I could see life going on all around me and I wanted to be part of it again. (OK, maybe I was a bit jealous too. Would it have hurt them to invite me to Finn's stag do when they all came to mine?) I didn't realise that the more time I spent with people's secrets, the more I'd grow to care about them. The thing that frightens me most isn't the grief I'm going to get, it's knowing the safety of others could depend on me. I could run away from it, but I wouldn't be able to respect myself ever again. So I'm making a promise: I will never let Lewis treat anyone like he treated Ruth. Just don't ask me how I can make sure of this. I don't know yet. All I know is I'm exhilarated and scared, like I was when I started all this. But from now on, it's for real.

Hollyoaks: Luke's Secret Diary

After 15 March 2000, Luke will never be the same again. Containing his intimate thoughts as he progresses from cocky wide-boy and star of the football field to rape victim, this is Luke's story in his own words.

ISBN 0 7522 7210 1 £3.99

Hollyoaks: The Lives And Loves Of Finn

Who is Finn: a convict's son? A man who would sleep with his mate's mum? Someone who'd cheat on his girlfriend? Or is he all of these…? This is the inside story of one of *Hollyoaks* most popular characters.

ISBN 0 7522 7211 X £3.99

Hollyoaks: Luke's Journal: A New Beginning

In this sequel to *Luke's Secret Diary* Luke is trying to pick up the pieces after the rape. But when the trial causes terrible repercussions for the Morgans, and Mandy wants to be just friends, he realises leaving the past behind him isn't that easy…

ISBN 0 7522 1954 5 £4.99

You can order copies direct from the Channel 4 Shop by calling **0870 1234 344**. Postage and packing is free in the UK.